REVENGE HAREM

ARTIE PFEIFFER

FIRED

"You're fired, Felix."

My head snapped up from the test plan that I'd be running.

"Excuse me?" I shook my head like I was getting water out of my ears. I couldn't possibly have heard my boss correctly.

"You're fired," Daphne said with relish. There was a hint of smugness in her eyes. "You need to clear out your cubicle and be out of here by 5 PM. Leave your card with security on your way out."

I swallowed hard as I watched her sashay out of my cubicle to her corner office. A year ago, she'd been a hot intern, one of three that I'd overseen for the summer. Six months ago, she'd married the CEO of our little startup right as the startup began to explode exponentially. Three months ago, Daphne had taken over the quality assurance division. Our CEO was too blind to force her to sign a prenup. She owned half of the company and acted like it. She hadn't been a terrible intern, a little green, but she was a terrible boss. She had no idea how things worked and also hated it when any of us tried to tell her how things functioned.

"You're the worst performing QAer," she said, putting on a sexy little sad pout, her lipstick blood red. "So sorry, we have to let you go."

"What about a performance improvement plan?" I asked, my heart sinking as she smirked down at me. I tried not to look at her cleavage. I had heard sounds coming out of her office which meant that she was sleeping around on the boss while he was on business trips. She was a man-eating wolf in sheep's clothing.

"Did Dan sign off on this?" Dan had hired me five years ago on a recommendation from his mentor, who'd taught me in class for a semester.

"Dan doesn't have to sign off on this. I own half of this company, remember?"

I got to my feet and started pulling stuff out of the drawers of my desk. "Fine. I'll be out by 5."

"Three," she corrected me.

"What? You said five." What was she talking about? Was this just a big power trip while her husband wasn't around?

"You want to make it 2?" We both looked at the clock. It was 15 minutes until 2 PM.

"Whatever," I said, my shoulders slumping. She had a bounce in her step as she walked away. I hated myself, but I couldn't stop from watching her sauntering away, her hips swinging in a tight and short skirt while she wore six-inch stilettos with red soles.

Within thirty minutes, I'd gathered everything from my gray cubicle. I heard whispers, especially from my work buddy Xavier's cubicle, as I walked to the security office near the exit. I surrendered my keycard and got a lecture on how IT would cut off my access at 5. They also gave me a bunch of information, such as directions to the unemployment office. I hated the look of pity in the security guard's eyes.

I couldn't even absorb the information while I stood there, just nodded my head once in a while. Finally they let me go. I drove home. The roads were empty because the school buses had already dropped all the kids off at home and everyone else was still at work.

I was unemployed.

DUMPED

*W*hen I got home, I noticed that Amber had parked her car in our slot, so I reversed out of the parking garage and parked outside. Maybe she was working from home today. Her boss seemed to be really lenient and she was forever asking me to leave the Midwest and fly off to Thailand. I didn't know if the pictures of pristine beaches were close to the reality that she'd painted for us. As soon as I climbed up the stairs and unlocked our front door, I heard moans.

"Oh, yeah, baby, right there!" she panted.

Fuck me. She was having sex. Without me.

I was paralyzed in place as I heard Amber's moans growing louder. She never moaned like that when she was around me. She always complained that I was too fast in the bedroom and needed to be more dominant. We'd done some bondage and stuff, but she always pushed for more. The truth was that I had some pretty hardcore fantasies, but I was afraid of going too far and having Amber leave me.

Amber was screaming now, which broke the spell holding me in place. I walked to our bedroom and looked at the people in bed. I was wrong. Partially, at least. Not all of the moans and screams had been from Amber. Our neighbor was in my bed. Our bed.

Our neighbor was a sexy, tiny Latina with huge brown eyes, curly hair, and the body of a fertility goddess, with tits and ass to spare. I was getting an eyeful of her body now and her smooth golden skin without any kind of tan lines. Bianca was 69ing my fiancée.

I couldn't get a good read on my own emotions. I was angry and hurt that Amber had betrayed me. I was already getting hard, though, just watching them go to town on each other. Amber's legs were shaking the way that they did when she was having a particularly good orgasm, the kind that meant that I'd wake up to a morning blow job the next day.

I tore myself away from the sight of Amber and Bianca. It felt like I was violating their privacy, even when they were doing it in the apartment that I paid the rent on. Amber was a consultant who was on the road two weeks of every month with two weeks in my apartment. She said since she was only around 50% of the time, she should pay 25% of the rent. I'd said that I'd just pay all of it and not bother to put her on the lease. In return, she covered all of our vacations with her hotel membership rewards.

I looked at the front door and thought about leaving. I could still hear them. I decided to walk out and leave them to it. I didn't know how to handle it. In the kind of video I only watched when I was sure that Amber wasn't around, I'd join them in bed. They'd greet me enthusiastically. But the fact that they were doing it around 3 PM meant that they wanted to make sure that I wasn't around.

Was it really a surprise that Amber was cheating on me? She was out of my league, a former beach volleyball player with sun-streaked blonde hair and a wide smile. She was the life of every party that she ever dragged me to. I'd normally spend them huddled in the corner with my phone and a single beer while she sat on other guys' laps. She knew I'd never break up with her. I'd imagined that she had some on the side, but I'd proposed to her a month ago when she started hinting that she needed commitment or she'd walk. An engagement ring was supposed to be three months of my salary, but the one that she'd chosen before I proposed was a year's worth of my salary before taxes. It looked good on her finger. I was worried that her expensive tastes might prove ruinous when we were married, but I'd cross that bridge when I got to it. I made a decent amount of money but she could suck me dry within a year if I was as dumb as my boss and went in without a prenup. I'd already mentioned going to a lawyer for a prenup to her, but she'd responded by giving me the silent treatment for two weeks. I still had to figure it out.

On some level, I understood why she was hooking up with Bianca. That curvy little Latina was fire and nearby. Amber worked from home for two weeks of every month. I didn't know what Bianca did, but she seemed to be around a lot. Maybe she worked the night shift somewhere. She baked stuff all the time and seemed to be constantly giving us cookies in some shape or form. You might think that a girl who ate that many cookies wouldn't be hot as fire, but Bianca had curves in all the right places. She wore a lot of low-cut shirts that showcased her breasts, even if Amber told me it was rude to stare. It was hard not to stare, although I'd gotten better at not getting caught.

Evidently Amber wasn't great at not getting caught, although I might never have learned the truth if I hadn't been fired out of the blue today. Taking the stairs back to the garage, I got in my car and drove aimlessly. Somehow, I ended up in front of my mom's house. She remarried and never seemed to have time for me because she and my stepdad were always traveling. She said that she'd taken care of me for long enough. I had to check the house once in a while to pick up mail and make sure the plants weren't dead, so I parked and started to look at things.

While I was turning on the hose so I could water the plants, I saw the twins next door sunbathing. While I watched one of them took off her top and talked to the other one. Giggling, the second one took off her top, too. I swallowed hard, but I couldn't tear my eyes off of them. The twins were my age. Our moms used to be really close, because they'd been roommates in college; I'd been around them for our whole lives. We had fun when we were kids but when we hit puberty and I had acne and a cracking voice, they'd turned into miniature goddesses and cheerleaders who didn't have time for me. It was hard not to be a little bit jealous about their position on top of the social ladder. They acted like they didn't even know my name anymore. I was embarrassing.

I'd founded a robotics club back then. I found my people. I didn't do much with it nowadays, because I was so busy, but maybe that'd change. At least robots were easy to understand. You programmed them to behave in a certain way and could calculate what you needed with simple math. If there was some kind of glitch, it was because of a logical error. I just wished that women were that simple.

OFFERING

*A*fter doing some chores around my mom's house, I got back into my car. It sounded like the twins were having some kind of splash fight in the pool, but I didn't look. It was hard to stare into the window of a bakery, smell the freshly baked goods, and never get a taste. They were both dating professional athletes, guys whose names were tossed around when people gathered at the water cooler. I didn't play a lot of sports growing up. I'd never been particularly good at them. So when people talked to me about the game, I pretended to know what was going on but in reality I had to watch the ESPN highlight reel before going to work.

Now that I was unemployed, I guessed that I wouldn't have to watch videos on ESPN anymore. I felt like going to a bar and having a drink. I went to a wing place around the corner from my childhood home and seated myself. A tall girl wearing a tight shirt came over to my table, her hair in a high ponytail. A nametag on her tits said EVELYNN. Her hair was down to her ass. She was wearing a lot of black makeup and chewing gum. "How can I help ya?" she asked. "Do you want to hear about our specials?"

I looked at the menu. "Nah, I'll just take some wings with buffalo sauce."

"Anything else? A drink?"

"What do you have on tap?"

She listed a few.

"What would you recommend?"

"It's kind of early in the day. With buffalo sauce, I'd probably go with our wheat ale. It's locally produced."

"Sounds good enough to me." One of my cousins was really into matching booze with food, but as long as they both tasted good, I could care less.

I stood up and picked up a game pad to play Texas Hold'em while I waited. I started owning the robots right before Evelynn came back with my food and flounced off. Her shirt was small enough and tight enough for me to see a couple inches of her bare lower back. Her hips flared from a tiny waist into hip-hugging jeans that made her ass look like something in a magazine. You know which kind.

I saw my order come out of the kitchen, but it just sat there while she complained about how much she hated her AP Stats teacher. She was in high school. I felt dumb for looking at jailbait and just waited for my food to come. An eternity later, she dropped it on my table without a word and was gone. There was no sauce on the chicken wings, just plain fried chicken. I looked around to ask her to bring sauce or something, but I had to resort to using the ketchup that was sitting at the table. Grumbling to myself, I promised that she wouldn't get a good tip.

The second that I put my last wing down, she swooped down on my table and gave me the check, not even in a folder.

"Have a nice day!" she said. She was already untying her apron. "I have to get to practice. Sheri will take care of you now. Bye."

She left in a hurry. I took out a bunch of cash and left a tip before going back to my car.

I didn't know where to go. I didn't want to go home and confront Amber. It was hot to watch her hook up with Bianca, but it was shitty that she'd snuck around behind my back. I didn't know how to deal with it yet, so I just went to the mall and walked around aimlessly.

"Hey!" I heard someone shout behind me. I turned and saw Gareth waving his arms at me. I hadn't seen Gareth since high school. "Hey man!" He walked up and shook my hand. "Long time no see."

I was stunned to see Gareth out of the blue. "Do you even live here?"

"What a question," Gareth laughed. "No, I'm just in town for a little while."

"Oh, cool," I replied, nodding. We looked at each other awkwardly for a moment.

"Listen, ah, I've been playing this new game and I think you'd love it."

I gave him side-eye. "What?" What the fuck was going on? He'd just said hello to me for the first time since high school, and he'd abruptly jumped to talking about some game. "I don't know..." I didn't really have time for video games right now, or from another perspective I had nothing but time for video games right now.

"There's this cool VR store in here. They have rigs like Oculus Rift but better."

"I've tried out an Oculus headset." I shrugged. "I wasn't that impressed."

"I promise you, it puts Oculus and Magic Leap to shame. Just try it once. The first time is free."

He sounded like a drug dealer. "I'm busy," I told him, even though I wasn't.

"Just for a few minutes," he said. I didn't understand why he was so adamant on getting me to try out this game.

"I gotta go," I responded. He took my sleeve and started pulling me down the hallway. I yanked on my sleeve and tore it. We both heard it rip. I looked at the piece of my shirt that was in his hand.

"Come on!" he said, a desperate note in his voice.

"What, are you a Jehovah's Witness or something now and have to help me see the light?" Something was wrong with him.

"Just a few minutes," he said. "You can walk away after that."

I shrugged and followed his lead. He was acting strangely. Maybe he really wanted some referral gems or something from bringing people into the game. When we went to a dark storefront that was painted black, I stopped. "It says that it's under construction."

"It's like a speakeasy," he explained. "You have to know the right word to get in."

I was creeped out by the unmarked storefront that had all of the windows covered in black. "Listen, I'm going to go."

This time, his hand gripped my wrist. He had freakish grip strength considering neither of us worked out. I knew what happened to my shirt. "Don't dislocate my wrist," I warned, trying to get free. His hand just tightened.

"Just a few minutes," he repeated like a robot.

It seemed that I didn't have much of a choice when he banged three times on the door. It opened and let us into a place that looked like a doctor's office. There was a blond man behind the counter.

"A newb named Felix," Gareth said to him, still dragging me forward.

I didn't get why a doctor's office would have blacked out windows. I didn't understand why a video game company would look like a doctor's office. Everything about this place felt off, but Gareth's hand was still on my wrist.

"Gareth, I'm going to go."

"Please, stay," the man behind the counter said, showing too many teeth when he smiled. "Can I get you a beer? Some wine?"

Free beer was okay by me any day of the week. "Uh, sure, just some Budweiser if you have it."

He pulled out a can of Budweiser and gave it to me.

"Are you a bartender or something?"

He chuckled. "Or something. Excuse me. Please make yourselves comfortable."

Gareth dragged me over to a couch and wouldn't let go of my wrist. "What the fuck, dude? Let go of my wrist."

"Just a few minutes," Gareth repeated.

My heart rate started to spike. I didn't drink the Budweiser. With my luck today, it'd turn out to have roofies in it or something. Plus I'd just had a beer at the wings place.

"Hi!" I heard a voice say behind me. I turned and felt my jaw drop.

Behind me was one of the cutest women I'd ever seen in my life. Evelynn the waitress might've been in high school, and the girl behind me looked like she was barely a freshman in college. "Uh, hi," I said, wondering if I'd put on cologne today.

"Come with me!" she chirped. Gareth finally let go of my wrist. He didn't have to force me to follow the girl into the back. When we walked, I noticed the sway of her perfect ass as she brought us to the back. She was wearing a blue dress that might as well have been spray-painted onto her perfect body. Watching the muscles of her legs move with every step in her sky-high heels was making my temperature rise a little. We went into a little office at the end of the hallway. She had eyes the color of her blue dress, porcelain skin, and an X-rated pout. She was the definition of flawless. She made my twin cheer-leading neighbors look like dried up old hags.

"I'm Luci with an I," she said, introducing herself. "Is there anything I can do to make you more comfortable?"

I shifted in my seat and thought about it. "Uh, no."

Gareth was nowhere near as tense as he had been out in the waiting room.

"How old are you?" I blurted out before I could stop myself. I felt my cheeks getting hot. "You look like..."

"I'm older than I look," she countered, fluttering her lashes at me. "But you're sweet."

I settled back in my chair. "Gareth said something about a VR world."

"Yes, we have some very new technology and we're looking for testers. We'll compensate you for your time by the hour." She named a number that was three times what I made per hour if you considered my salary to be divided by 2000 hours per year at the job that I'd left today. And considering I worked for a software company, I made a number well above the median American income. I used to, anyway.

"Sign me up," I interrupted.

"I thought you'd say that." She pushed a clipboard across the desk. "Go ahead and take a look. Ask me questions about anything that you don't understand."

I held the clipboard over the tent in my pants. It seemed like the average legalese that you had to sign whenever you started any new job. "You offer long-term immersion VR rigs?"

"Yes, we do. And you're a perfect candidate to put into one of them. You're a healthy, young male, the exact target audience of our product."

I scanned the lines of gibberish, but they had no meaning to me. I just signed everywhere that there was an X and put my initials where there was a highlighted field.

"Perfect!" Luci said. She grabbed the clipboard and pulled the papers out of the clip at the top. She shoved it into a drawer. "So we can get you started. We pay on a weekly basis."

"That's cool." I was distracted by how her boobs had bounced when she yanked the clipboard away from me. I didn't think she was wearing a bra at all. The dress showed her hard nipples poking through the thin fabric.

"Are you cold?" I asked her.

"No," she answered me. She eye-fucked me for a half second, a half smile on her lips. I swallowed hard and willed my erection to go away. I had to think about something else than titty-fucking her and giving her the best facial of her life. "Why don't you follow me into one of our open rooms?"

I stood up, pulling my shirt down a little to cover my boner. She smelled like cinnamon and something else that I couldn't place. We walked into one of the rooms that we'd passed in the hallway. It was brightly lit.

"So you've signed all of our consent forms and we'll set you up on our payroll system really soon," she said, tossing her hair. The scent of her shampoo filled the room. It smelled like freshly cut roses. "And you'll just be in the system and have a lot of fun!"

Gareth had stayed in her office. I was on my own now. I put on the helmet and could feel her lightly touching me all over my body to set up the sensors. I felt her soft touch on my stomach, which made my hips buck. But she backed away, all professional now.

"You'll go through a brief introductory video and tutorial so that you know how to use the game," she said. I could still hear her even though my helmet was on. "Good luck. You can stay in there for as long as you need to. We'll take care of you out here." She must have flipped some kind of switch as soon as she stopped talking, because I could see some kind of intro sequence playing out in front of me.

INTRODUCTION AND AMBER

*S*he was the face of the tutorial video. "Hello, my name is Luci and I'm here to walk you through the game to maximize your pleasure." She gave the camera a saucy wink, as if she could see me directly through the head-set/helmet that I was wearing.

"Here's how you access your inventory. We start you out with a starter pack of coins and crystals, but you have to earn them within the game." She threw a gold coin at me which almost bounced off of my hand before I bought it. "Gold coins are the most valuable and are worth 100 bronze coins. A silver coin is worth 10 bronze coins. Got it?"

There was a little question mark floating in front of me with two options: yes or no. Because I had successfully completed elementary school, I could do that much math. I clicked yes by reaching out and hitting it with my left hand.

"Now you know how to interact with the quests and the informational prompts provided," Luci continued. All of a sudden, her avatar lost its clothes, leaving her in skimpy lingerie that was totally see-through, showing off her pink nipples. Continuing like she wasn't giving me the show of my life, she turned to an icon on the bottom right-hand corner. The thong she was wearing basically exposed 99% of her perfect ass. "This icon is your wardrobe." She pulled a black robe out of the closet, looking something like what the cast of Harry Potter wore in the films when they were at Hogwarts if the girls wore robes that had collars that almost revealed their belly buttons. She slipped it on and twirled, letting the bottom fly around her. I could still see the band of her lacy bra, which had a tiny ribbon bow in the center.

"Now you." She motioned for me to click the wardrobe icon and pull out some clothes.

"Uh, why is there only a white sheet?"

"It's for your toga, nerd," she informed me as if it were totally obvious. They had some good AI in this game. "You have to buy clothes unless you want to go naked.

I pushed for the game to start out with everyone naked, but I got vetoed." She rolled her eyes and tapped her foot. "I don't have all day, you know."

The tutorial was kind of sassy. I made a note to tell the devs to turn down the attitude before I pulled the sheet around me and did a half-hearted toga that I hoped would stay put until I could figure out where in the game I could get more clothes for my wardrobe.

"Great!" Luci continued. "Now I should show you your questbook." She leaned down, letting me see a generous amount of cleavage from that angle. I put my tongue back in my mouth as I reached for my questbook.

"Here's where you accept all the quests," she told me. "Go ahead and hit accept for your first quest."

TUTORIAL
Finish being taught basic actions in the game by Luci.

I clicked accept, which made the quest move from the bottom to the main quest area.

"Get out of your questbook, dork," Luci said. She was really kind of mean for AI. I hit the X button in the top corner and got back into the main view.

"Now, every newb starts out as a knight. You got a wooden sword and shield at the beginning." They showed up and automatically put themselves into a little rectangle that showed the slots for my gear. "As you progress in the game, you'll get better weapons, or so I hope. Don't fuck it up."

She started walking at a pace that forced me to walk pretty fast to catch up with her.

"Where are we going?"

"The witch's house," she replied. We kept going until we went around a corner and I saw a small shack.

"I don't know if I want to go in there." I felt a little trepidation. She was just a pre-recorded AI tutorial version of Luci, but she rolled her eyes at me and pushed the door open. I hesitated outside for about two seconds before following her inside.

It smelled like potions had been brewing for about a thousand years inside. It was musty. It was humid. Everything was awful. I covered my nose and tried to breathe through my mouth, but it just made everything worse. I made another mental note to tell them that the smell for the first location was way too strong. I didn't understand how they'd made it so realistic, but I was not a fan of this place. I didn't know if they wanted to chase off their customers or what, but the witch's house needed to be reworked.

"Welcome to my home, young knight," the witch cackled. Luci was sitting in a corner playing with a black cat. "Are you ready to accept a quest?"

"Uh, sure," I said, sneaking a glance at Luci who wasn't paying any attention to me. She seemed to care way more about giving the cat a good belly rub as the cat tried to bat at the ribbon between Luci's tits. I opened my questbook.

SEVEN APPLES
The witch has a potion that is almost

complete. Go to her garden and find seven ripe apples so she can complete it.

I hit accept. It moved to the right part of my questbook.

"Here's why I leave you," Luci said, standing up even though the cat was now angry at her and very offended that she had the audacity to stop playing with it. "You've finished your tutorial. I've shown you the wardrobe, questbook, gear, money, and more. If you need to learn more about things or didn't pay attention the first time, just hit the little information button and it'll explain itself to you."

"I got it," I said.

"Good luck. I'll see you in a bit." Luci waved goodbye and disappeared in a puff of red smoke.

"She left you to me," the witch snickered. "Go into my garden and find the apples."

I walked to the door under the angry gaze of the witch's cat. I realized then that her garden was fucking huge. I imagined it to be the kind of garden that you got in a suburban household when you grew a few flowers outside or something. No. It was like a farm out there.

"How am I supposed to find apples?" I asked myself. I didn't see any fruit trees at all. The quest had seemed simple when I accepted it. I stood around for a minute before realizing I was just going to have to search for things on foot. I didn't get the impression that the witch was supposed to give me more specific instructions. I made another mental note about it. At this point, I was going to have to tell them to put a notebook function into the game.

I started to walk in one direction. At least they hadn't put any insects in the game. I was approaching a bunch of trees that would make me spray myself with Deep Woods OFF if I encountered it in real life. I was only wearing a toga, too, which didn't help things. I kept walking until I saw a bunch of apple trees. Then I realized that I was going to have to put the apples into my inventory. I started picking a bunch. I didn't know if I needed to eat inside of the game, but I thought about bad things happening in myths to people who ate things that they didn't have permission to eat. Maybe this second quest was some kind of test. I wasn't hungry because of whatever they'd hooked me up to, so I just gathered the apples, dumped them into my inventory, and hightailed it back to the witch's home.

By the time I got there, the stench had spread from her home into the air around it. It was strong enough to make my eyes water.

"I brought back 7 ripe apples."

"Good," she said. "Give them here." I put the apples into her hands. She cast them into the cauldron that was bubbling in the hearth.

"Did you eat any?" she asked.

"No." So it was a test. There was some kind of notification that showed up showing that I'd completed SEVEN APPLES.

"Good." She stirred the concoction in silence for a minute. "For your self-restraint, you'll be rewarded. I will give you three apples."

"Uh, thanks?" I didn't know if I wanted to eat poisoned apples or whatever she was doing in the hearth.

She laughed at me. "You don't know what the apples do, idiot boy."

I didn't, so I stayed quiet.

"They're Apples of Discord. They cause chaos if they're tossed into the center of a bunch of people. Remember, you can't use this if you're isolated. It's a good cover for escape. They'll become more important as you progress. By the way, you're no longer a knight."

"I'm not?" Luci had just said that everyone started as a knight.

"You're a baronet now. The land that you walked is now yours."

I didn't know if I wanted to be so close to the witch's home, but I guess that they had designed the game to be like this. "Okay."

"The next level is baron." She pursed her lips. "Choose one of the homes on my table." She gestured with her left hand and made a bunch of tiny model homes appear on the table.

I inspected them. When I was a kid, my art class had done a field trip to a museum of miniature houses. She could make them show up out of thin air. All of them seemed to be one story with the basics inside. I chose one that reminded me of the house I'd grown up in.

"Keep it in your pocket until you find a water source. Then put it in the water and watch the magic happen."

"What does that mean?"

She only shook her head. "You'll see. Here, take three Apples of Discord."

I took the glistening apples from her hand. They definitely weren't the same apples that I'd picked from the tree. I put them into my inventory. I put the house into it, too.

"Now go and set up your caput." My questbook had a little red notification on it. I clicked on it.

SET UP HOUSE
Find a place on your land to place your caput.

I didn't know what she was talking about, but I walked back in the direction of the apple tree that I'd picked apples from. Maybe this entire region was considered the witch's garden. She'd said that the land was mine, though, so I just went in the same direction and stopped next to a tiny creek. I stopped myself from putting the house in the middle of the woods. If I was going to set up a home, I'd probably want some kind of lake. I kept walking for another hour, working up a sweat. When I was about to give up, turn around, and go back to the creek, I found a huge, empty lake. I took the house out of the inventory and set it into the water. It immediately began to expand. I leapt out of the way as it just exploded. I pushed it a little further onto land. The last thing I wanted was a soggy house.

It was approximately the size of a one-room log cabin. "I guess that's my caput." I shrugged. I didn't understand what a caput was. I remembered that Luci had said something about being able to click information buttons, so I hunted for any kind of button. Finally, I realized that there was one on the front door. I hit it with my hand.

CAPUT

House belonging to Felix the Baron. If captured, becomes property of conquerer and the owner becomes a vassal of the conqueror.

It seemed kind of intense and scary. I didn't know about the feudal system other than some kind in AP Euro in high school. I didn't want to be anybody's vassal. There were other games where people waited around for the newbies to walk in and robbed them blind. I hoped they didn't do that, or I'd X out of this game so fast my head would spin. How did I turn the game off?

Then I realized that Luci had never told me how to get out of the game. I hunted around all of my menus and options, but there was no LOG OFF option. My heart rate began to spike as I realized that she'd told me to finish the game and take all the time I needed to. I looked for any kind of communication system that'd go back to HQ. Nothing. Fuck. I was stranded in the game until I finished the whole thing. I had a wooden sword that would prevent exactly zero people from conquering me. It could probably give someone a splinter if it came down to it. That someone would probably be me.

I took the sword and shield out of my inventory and started to practice with them. I regretted not taking fencing lessons in the real world, but in most video games, the avatar did the fighting.

You just had to learn what attacks you had. I looked for anything that would show me my abilities. I came up empty. It seemed that I actually had to fight with a useless sword and shield. I pressed the float information button.

"Hi!" Luci said, appearing in a cloud of red smoke.

"How am I supposed to defend myself with these?" I brandished the sword and shield. "I'm going to be someone else's vassal the first time someone comes to my little barony and takes over my house."

"New players get automatic protection while they get on their feet." Luci put two fingers in her mouth and gave an ear-piercing whistle. Immediately a big black dog came running at us. It was a really good-looking dog, if I had to say so. I liked dogs.

"Here, boy," I said, extending my hand for the dog to sniff and trying not to make eye contact as we fought for alpha status. The dog sniffed my hand and then pounced on me, pinning me to the ground while it enthusiastically licked my face.

Getting your face licked by a normal dog was bad enough, but this dog smelled like rotten eggs and burned things. It kept licking my face even as I tried to get away. I could hear Luci's mocking laughter.

"How classic," she sniggered. "It never gets old." She cleared her throat. "You're issued a hellhound for your first three days, but during that time, you need to obtain Guardians."

"Guardians?" I asked.

"Your harem, of course." She acted like it was totally obvious.

"Uh, what?" I was disoriented and had a dog weighing approximately a thousand pounds on top of me while I smelled its rotten breath. Did they make mouth-wash for digital dogs? And why were the smells in this game so strong and real?

"You have to obtain ladies for your harem."

"How do I do that?" I couldn't even move, let alone convince NPCs to enter my harem.

"It's catered to you and based on your own life," Luci explained. "They are all women you know."

"So like... people in the real world show up here?"

"More like you show up there. Your hell-hound will guard your caput while you get the first members of your harem."

"Can't I just stay here?" I asked.

"No," she giggled. "Get offa him, Rufus." The hound snuffled before getting off of me. I wiped the saliva off with my sleeve. "You have to finish the game, remember?"

"Oh yeah."

"So you started out as a knight. You became a baronet when you walked and claimed the land. Now you've placed your caput here and are a baron. But this is the last of the easy levels."

Wandering around in the wilderness while having zero clue of what the fuck I was supposed to do was easy? Oh, fuck. "What's after being a baron?"

"You become a Laird o Pairlament, of course."

"Of course," I echoed. "Laird o what?"

"It's Scottish, silly. The game designers took inspiration from a lot of different places. Scottish barons are minor nobility because they are the heads of prescriptive baronies. There are actually shades of ranking within the Scottish barons, but we didn't want to confuse the American audience too much. So after you become a baron, you ascend to becoming a Laird o Pairlament instead of going through a tedious rise of shades of being a Scottish feudal baron, become a lord or earl or whatever." She twirled her long white-blonde hair around one finger. "By the way, the three days started when I gave the hellhound to you, so the clock is ticking."

"What... how do I get my first Guardian?" I asked.

"It's based on your life," Luci yawned. "Whatever, you've completed the first quest. Tutorial done. Tata for now." She disappeared in another cloud of red smoke.

I saw some XP notification float in the corner of my screen before it vanished. I didn't know what the levels meant, because apparently I was progressing by finishing quests. It'd really help if I had some straightforward guidance. I touched the questbook again.

PICK UP YOUR FIRST GUARDIAN
Overcome her obstacles in order to obtain her trust and loyalty.

Uh, okay. I didn't know what it meant, but I accepted the quest anyway. It must have been triggered when Luci had marked the tutorial quest as complete. Suddenly, my surroundings changed. I was nowhere near my caput and borrowed hellhound. Instead, I was in my apartment. What the fuck was happening? I could see the bed was just like it was when I had left my home earlier that day. If I sniffed a little, I could smell what Bianca and Amber had been up to.

"Babe?" I asked experimentally.

"Felix!" I heard Amber say. "Give me a minute, I'm getting out of the shower now."

She emerged from the bathroom wearing a towel that didn't quite cover the tops of her thighs. I could see her pussy peeking out. Like always, my train of thought derailed like a subway car speeding on a broken track.

"Hey babe," Amber said, grinning at me. She leaned forward and gave me a kiss on the cheek. "Was work good?"

I didn't know what to say and was distracted by the smell of her shampoo. Our bathroom always smelled great when she got out of the shower. I didn't know how the game developers had gotten things to be so realistic, but I just rolled with it. Inside of the game, did I have to tell her the truth? In this reality, had I been fired by Daphne?

"I'm not working there anymore," I told her. "As of today."

I could see surprise and concern flicker across her pretty face. "But how are you going to afford our wedding?"

"Babe, I couldn't afford what you planned even when I had a job. We're going to have to scale down or something."

"Scale down?" she screeched, her face flushing. "What, like use disposable napkins instead of cloth ones?"

"Probably cut down on the guest list."

"The invitations have already gone out," she spat, her face an unhealthy shade of red. "Are we going to uninvite your side of the family?"

Outside of the game, I was afraid of Amber leaving me. I knew I couldn't do better and that I was a lucky bastard to have her at all. Hypergamy was real, and on some level I expected her to ditch me. But knowing that this whole thing was just a simulation based on stuff in my mind without any real world consequences gave me the courage to push back. "We could uninvite yours."

"I fucking hate you!" she screamed. She went to the couch, bent over, flashed a little bit of her ass at me as the towel went up, and threw a pillow at me. "You're ruining everything."

"I haven't ruined anything. You're the one who is cheating on me."

"What?" she sputtered. "I'm not cheating on you. I'd never cheat on you. We're getting married."

"Then why does our bed still smell like Bianca?" Bianca always smelled like baked goods. I thought that she was obsessed with baking. "Tell me if I walk into our bedroom right now, I won't smell her."

Amber dropped her towel. "You're the only one I have eyes for, baby," she cooed. She was trying to distract me, and it was working. Amber had naturally perfect breasts, her best feature. She had dusky rose nipples and pure white skin, which was only marred by a few bite marks.

"Bianca left marks," I pointed out. I touched one of her breasts. "There are bite marks."

I didn't know that it was even possible for Amber to turn any redder, but she did. "I'm not sure what you mean. They're from you."

I was tired of her lying to me. Wanting evidence, I waved my hand and showed up in Bianca's apartment. She was taking something out of the oven and putting it on a cooling rack. I could smell the wonderful scent of peanut butter cookies. Bianca was generous when it came to sharing baked goods, and the peanut butter cookies she made had chocolate in the center. My mouth was watering.

"Bianca," I said, hitting the new PHEROMONES button that said it was supposed to put pheromones into the air. I didn't think I was close enough, though, so I came closer. The oven was still open when she turned and saw me.

"How did you get in?" Bianca asked. Then I saw her nose twitch. She sneezed a little, a confused look on her face. Then some unholy light was shining from her eyes.

"You..." she said, drooling a little. "When did you get so hot?"

I smiled a little. There hadn't been much of a guide to this game, but I could see that her pupils were dilated. She came up to me, and as if she couldn't help herself, started rubbing my abs.

"I need to..." she whispered, before sinking to her knees and unzipping my pants. In real life, I probably would've been startled enough to flinch away from a hot girl just sticking my cock in her mouth. Inside of the game, I watched as she took my cock out of my pants and started coaxing it to full hardness with her tongue. I could see that she was much more experienced with oral sex than Amber. I braced myself on the kitchen counter while she went to town. I wound my hands through her silky stick straight black hair. She was moaning around my cock like it was the best sexual experience she'd had in her life. I would bet that if I stuck my fingers inside of her, she'd be wetter than the ocean. I felt my muscles contract and tapped her shoulder right before I came in her mouth. On the rare occasions that Amber could be convinced to give me head, she spit. Bianca was swallowing like my semen was ambrosia, the nectar of the gods. With my semen just barely leaking out of her mouth, I waved my hand and took us back into my apartment, caressing her soft hair.

"I'm done with your lies," I said, my tone cold and Bianca still at my feet, clearly just having blown me. Amber was backing away from me now, but our apartment wasn't big enough for her to get far. "You've been cheating with other people. Is Bianca it, or are there other people?"

She looked to her left. "Um."

"You've been fucking multiple people while you're in town. Are you cheating on me when you travel?" Bianca was eyeing my cock like she wanted more, paying no attention to the woman she'd fucked earlier today.

"Of course," Amber spat. Her eyes were full of anger. "You think that you're enough to satisfy me? Please. I'm only with you because I think you'll be a good dad. You'll stay at home with our kids, manage the boring stuff, and not bother me too much. You know that you're lucky to have me."

I looked at her naked body and the marks on her skin. I was somehow clinically detached, acknowledging that she was way hotter than I was. "Your sassy attitude ends today," I warned her.

"Get the fuck out of here before I call the cops!" she tossed back.

"It's my apartment. You aren't even on the lease. You don't pay any rent." I had to push Bianca away from my dick as she tried to dive for it again. Those pheromones had been pretty powerful. I decided that Bianca didn't need to witness the argument Amber and I were having, so I made her disappear in a cloud of red smoke. I hadn't used the pheromones on Amber yet, but if Bianca was any indication, letting her have a whiff of them would result in good things.

"And you won't, either, since you don't have a job anymore."

"Don't be fucking stupid," I threw back. "I have savings."

I could see the surprise in her face. "You have..."

"More money than you've been able to sink your hands into? Yeah. I can make a hardship withdrawal from my 401k if I really need it, but I have cash sitting in an account and investments sitting around. If you were married to me, you'd have a right to them. But since you won't be marrying me, it's not a concern."

"Not marrying you?" she spluttered.

"You just threatened to call the cops on me."

"You just did something bad to Bianca."

"Bianca loved every second of it and she was the one who initiated it." Sort of. "You're a bitch," I responded. "And I'm not afraid of any cops." Considering that I could apparently disappear in a cloud of red smoke inside of the game, I wasn't worried about being locked up or hurting Amber. I'd never raised a hand to any woman before, besides the time when I was five and tussling about who got to take the next turn on the swings. I'd gotten into such bad trouble then that I'd never repeated the experience, plus she'd kicked my ass and I had bruises for a few weeks after that playground fight. I'd had to transfer classrooms at my preschool, too, so my mom had been really stressed out about it. "What do you even get out of cheating? A thrill?"

"Better sex," she said. I could see from the triumph in her eyes that she intended for the remark to hurt me.

"It's not like you're a great lay," I told her. "You make me do all the work and just expect everything to be done for you."

"That's not true! I blow you... sometimes."

"You blow me on my birthday," I corrected her. "It's once a year, and frankly I don't know why I put up with you. You don't pay rent, you're frigid in bed, and you're cheating on me all the time anyway."

"Fine," Amber said, turning to the bedroom. "I'll pack and get out of your hair."

I sat down on my couch while I listened to Amber pack. When she started crying, I went into the bedroom. She was sitting in front of her suitcase, crying her eyes out. She was still naked.

"Why are you crying?" I was still mad at her, but it was still hard for me to watch any woman cry.

"I don't know where else I can go," she whispered.

"Bianca looked pretty friendly with you just a little while ago," I snarked. "It's not far, either."

"Bianca lives in an apartment paid for by a man three times her age," Amber said.

I had no idea that she was a sugar baby or whatever they called that kind of relationship these days. "So she's what, a prostitute?"

"Get your mind out of the gutter!" Amber yelped, scrambling to her feet. She seemed unconcerned with her nudity, so I got an eyeful of her gorgeous breasts bouncing from the sudden motion. "She has a generous boyfriend, that's all. But I can't stay with her."

"Because he visits Bianca. Probably with his walker and wearing some kind of heart rate monitoring device to make sure sex doesn't kill him."

"I don't know why you're like this," Amber said, her mouth turning down in a pouty frown that had changed the tide of too many of our fights to count. Even though I was angry at her, I couldn't help getting hard again. Now I was thinking about having Amber give me a blowjob like Bianca just had. "You're being so mean."

"I've had enough of your shit," I told her. "I cook. I clean. I pay the rent while you get to travel wherever your job takes you. You ask for things that are too expensive for us, but you get them anyway and I bring my lunch to work most of the time. I save so that you can spend my money, and it stops today. Why don't you just use your hotel points and stay somewhere for free? You can apartment hunt tomorrow."

"You're such a fucking asshole," Amber hissed. "I get no notice and suddenly I'm out on the street."

"Don't be ridiculous," I retorted. "You are acting as if I am kicking you out, but you're the one who cheated. You don't even care about it."

"Maybe if you kept me happier, we wouldn't be having this conversation."

"Maybe if you weren't a fucking slut who couldn't keep her legs closed, we wouldn't be having this conversation."

Amber was crying really hard now, her whole body shuddering with huge heaves. I felt like a dick, even if I knew that I had to put everything on the table. I really was done with her shit. She was the one who put us in this situation. I didn't ask for that much. I took care of everything, and it still wasn't enough for her. She'd still cheated on me with our neighbor and an unknown number of guys and girls.

"I just wish I could take it back."

"Take what?"

"All of it," she said, sobbing. Flinging herself at me, she curled her body around mine and sobbed into my shoulder. My anger kind of cooled off and despite everything, I knew I was even harder when I felt her tits pressing against me. "I'm so scared of what my mom will say when we cancel the wedding."

I slid my hand up her back, intending to comfort her. But I thought that I misjudged the distance, because somehow my hand ended up on her ass. I slid my hand downward, pinching her round curves.

"Hey!" she said, lifting her head and wiping away her tears. "Is it really appropriate for you to be groping me while we're breaking up?"

"Hate sex," I explained before picking her up, walking, and throwing her on the bed. Before she could react, I was pulling her legs apart. She might not have liked to go down on me, but I loved going down on her. She tasted like lemon drizzle cake. I could and actually did eat her for hours. The sounds she made and her wild hips turned me on a lot. Right now was no exception. She was arching, bucking, and moaning my name. She had her hands on the back of my head as she came close to climaxing. Amber was quick off the mark and could go for hours, which was one of the best things about her. I put two fingers into her cunt, which made her scream. I knew how to drive her crazy by circling and licking her clit. I was in imminent danger of a concussion from Amber, but I was okay with it.

"No more," she panted, tapping the bed-sheets like a wrestler would. "I can't come anymore." She was as boneless as a jellyfish beneath me. I wiped her taste off of my chin. "Why don't we do this more often?"

"Because I don't break up with you on a daily basis," I informed her.

I ruined the post-orgasm glow she had going on. She got into a sitting position and put a pillow in front of her, hugging it and looking like she'd cry again.

"I just want to work things out," she said. "It's going to be humiliating to explain to my family and friends why we broke up."

"You can lie and say that it was a mutual agreement that we weren't right for each other. Or you could tell them the truth, that you're a cheating whore and tossed it around like it was free."

"I'm not a cheating whore."

"You're a cheater, at the very least."

She didn't have a quick comeback for that. It was true, and we both knew it. I looked at the suitcase on the floor. It was half-full of her clothes. She kept a carry-on fully packed with two weeks of clothing, so she had random shit tossed into her big suitcase. Some of her stuff was still in a storage unit near her old apartment. She really meant to leave.

I didn't know if I felt relieved or upset that Amber was going out the door. A little bit of both, I guessed. We'd spent years together. I imagined a future with her. And now it was all gone because she couldn't keep her legs closed.

Amber went into the bathroom and cleaned up. I could hear the water running. I waited on my bed, still fully clothed. I could smell her scent in the air. When she was gone, it would slowly fade. So would Bianca's smell. I wondered if her sugar daddy knew Bianca wasn't exclusive. I wondered if he cared what Bianca did when he wasn't around.

Amber came out of the restroom, this time without a towel, because her was still on the floor next to the bed.

"Get dressed," I commanded her. Pouting, Amber bent down and shrugged into a dress without a bra or underwear. I could see her nipples poking through the thin fabric of whatever flowery print the dress had. She went to our shared closet and started pulling more stuff out. I wondered if anybody would care that Amber was a habitual cheater when she found her next victim. Probably not. She knew how to target the people who found her irresistible and knew they couldn't do any better than Amber. It was how she maintained control and power in the relationship. If she were dating Brad Pitt or something, she wouldn't know how to deal with it.

I went into the bathroom to take my own shower. I didn't understand why I felt sticky and sweaty inside the rig, but the water didn't seem to do me any harm. Showering made me feel better in the real world, too. When I got out, I saw that Amber was zipping up her suitcase. She wasn't crying anymore. Her hair was swept into a bun with a sparkly thing around it.

"So this is goodbye," she announced, her voice low and husky with tears.

"Goodbye," I told her. I'd be better off without this manipulative bitch.

She was frozen in place. "Are you sure?"

"I'm pretty damn sure," I replied. "I'll even carry your suitcase to the elevator like the gentleman I'm not." She still wasn't moving. "Why aren't you leaving? Don't let the door hit you on the way out."

Amber started shaking. I hadn't seen her have a panic attack too many times, but she got really antsy before flying. Stupid when her job required so much traveling but she'd been in a plane that had flown in terrible weather one time, and she had flashbacks and nightmares about it. She said that it felt like swatted around by the mighty hand of Zeus during a thunderstorm. She was already starting to hyperventilate.

On one hand, she could be putting on a show to stay in my apartment, formerly our apartment. On the other hand, I knew what a panic attack looked like, and she was in the beginning stages.

"Amber," I soothed her, running my hand through her silky smooth dark hair. "You're going to be okay. I can call any hotel you want and I'll even get an Uber on your phone to go there." Fuck me, I was way too nice sometimes, but it wasn't like I wanted her to die on the street or anything like that.

"I can't call my mom and tell her. She'll freak out," Amber whispered, looking like she was on the verge of tears. Her breaths were coming in quick little gasps.

"I'll call her," I volunteered and immediately berated myself in my head. Stupid! She was just manipulating me again.

"Can you take the blame?" she asked.

"I'll tell her the truth, that you cheated and we had to call it off." I reached for her cell phone, but she snatched it away from me.

"Don't!" she screamed. Her face went pale.

"You did the crime. Now do the time," I said. "Hand it over. You wanted me to call your mom."

"Yeah, but not like that!" she screeched, keeping the phone close. "I'll call her later." She was starting to hyperventilate.

"Whatever." I actually got along with her mom, maybe because Amber was way nicer when her mom was around. Her mom had a fantastic sense of humor and cracked me up. I was a little sad that I wouldn't be marrying into her family anymore, but if Amber was part of the package, I was better off in the long run.

"She likes you so much," Amber whispered, covering her eyes. "She thinks you're the only decent guy I've ever dated. She's seriously going to kill me."

"You should've thought of that before you were 69ing Bianca."

Amber's cheeks went completely white, whiter than before, and she was pale to begin with. "You saw that?" she squeaked.

"Baby, I saw everything." I hadn't, but I'd been standing there long enough to see a lot of what she was up to when I wasn't home. "It was hot, to tell you the truth, but considering you were cheating on your fiancé at the time, I couldn't appreciate it as much as I otherwise would have."

"You thought it was hot?" She had

stopped crying and was wiping away her tears with the backs of her hands.

"Well, yeah." Wasn't it every guy's fantasy to hook up with two hot women at the same time?

"Maybe I could..." She stared at her feet and sighed, "I don't know."

"Are you suggesting that you put on a show for me?" I wasn't exactly going to turn it down. I hadn't seen much of her and Bianca, after all, just a few moments.

Amber hugged herself. "Is the wedding still off?"

"Why don't you put on a show, and we'll talk about things after." It wasn't a question. I'd already told her to get out, but watching two girls go at it in my bed wasn't something I was going to pass up.

I snapped my fingers. Bianca had the tray of cookies in her hands, like she knew I'd want them when she re-entered my apartment.

"Sustenance?" she asked, offering the tray to me. "The cookies aren't too hot for you, my lord."

I reached for one of them and bit into it. It was the perfect temperature, where it was hot enough for the chocolate to melt but cool enough to eat. The smell of peanut butter was now filling my apartment. I saw Amber's eyes on the tray, as if she wanted to have some.

"Take one of these cookies," I told Bianca. She obediently took one of them off of the cookie tray and looked like she was about to eat it. "No, it's not for you." I could see confusion in Bianca's eyes, but her mouth closed. "It's for Amber." I took the warm tray from Bianca's hands and put it on our stovetop. "Go lay down on the couch on your back, thighs apart."

Bianca scrambled to the couch, spreading her thighs so far apart that she was half off of the couch. It wasn't all that wide, which would put a damper on Amber going down on her. I snapped my fingers to make the couch into a futon that had already been spread out.

"What the fuck!" Amber yelped.

"On your knees," I told her. I pointed at Bianca.

Amber hadn't been hit by the same dose of pheromones. Everything she was doing was up to her. Slowly, she sank to her knees, although her face still showed some apprehension.

"Balance the cookie on top of your pussy, sweetheart," I commanded Bianca. She put the cookie in the right spot and arched her back, a low moan in the back of her throat.

"Eat her. Eat it," I instructed Amber.

Still moving slowly, Amber's head bent down. I saw her hand come up to grab the cookie.

"No hands," I corrected her.

I watched as she had to chase the cookie all over the juncture of Bianca's thick and muscular thighs. I frankly didn't know how Bianca spent her time, but she looked like she could ride someone until the break of dawn. I stroked myself slowly as I watched Amber's tongue dart out and try to eat the cookie while going down on Bianca. I wished I had some chocolate whipped cream.

And then abruptly, I had a can of chocolate whipped cream in my hand. This game was pretty neat. They had to read my mind somehow. I knew that they were drawing from my memories, but the wish that I'd just made wasn't part of most of my memories. It had only occurred to me because it seemed appropriate for the situation at hand, with peanut butter cookies with chocolate in the center. Amber was licking up the crumbs as Bianca writhed beneath her when I pulled Amber's hair to take her away from Bianca's cookie. Cookies, if I were being honest.

"What?" she barely had the time to get out as I sprayed some of the whipped cream on my dick. In another second, I was pushing it down her throat, almost hard enough to drill a hole in it.

"No hands," I reminded her. With my hands in her hair and Amber kneeling still, she didn't have a lot of control in the situation. I saw Bianca, who had left a wet spot on the couch, get up from the couch as if she were sleepwalking and then kneel behind Amber.

"Master says no hands," she said as she took Amber's hands and held her wrists together. "No hands."

It was hot to watch Bianca restrain Amber. Yeah, Amber had agreed to this, but still. I didn't know why the game was into two chicks fucking each other and me, and I wasn't sure what the quest meant. But all of that flew out the window when Amber managed to make me come. I was skull-fucking her at that point, not really able to hold back. When I exploded in her mouth, I gave her no other option but to swallow my load or asphyxiate. I could see her throat frantically working to take it all down. Her face was turning red.

When I was done, I pulled out of her mouth. Amber was gasping hard for air. I could see how hard her nipples had gotten. My dirty freak of a former fiancée liked it. A lot, if the smile on her face was anything to judge by. I told Bianca, "Clean her up."

"Of course, Master," Bianca replied. She took Amber's hand and helped her to her feet. Then they went into the shower together. In a minute, I'd join them and make sure they were very clean. But I touched my questbook while the girls were otherwise occupied.

Infuriatingly, the quest was still not done. "What do I need to do in order to finish this quest?" I mumbled to myself. I didn't need exact instructions, but a hint would be nice. I could hear squeals and giggles coming from the bathroom. I'd have to play this part of the game again. It was a lot of fun. I knew that I'd cleared the first few levels from what Luci had said about baronets or whatever. The quest was still red, though, so I put it out of my mind and went into the bathroom.

Instead of opting for a quick 5-minute shower like I normally did in the mornings, the girls had gone into the bathtub. It was actually a giant bathtub and there was some kind of fancy name for it on the marketing materials for the apartment containing the word "garden." They were splashing each other. Ordinarily, I'd be annoyed because whenever Amber made a mess in the bathroom and made the floor too slippery for safety, I was the one who had to mop up everything. But inside this game, the floor was pleasantly warm and only slightly wet even though they'd been splashing each other for a while. I made sure I was ready to jump into the tub and then I did.

The water was the perfect temperature. I liked my water hotter than Amber did. She said that I tried to boil myself alive when I was in the shower and always complained that I used up the hot water, even though we lived in an apartment complex that had enough hot water for everyone in it. She and Bianca had soaped themselves up and were splashing each other in the garden tub. Their skin was glistening. I took a moment to admire how utterly desirable both of them looked with their hair down and soap bubbles sliding down their bodies.

"Felix!" Amber said right before she splashed me, getting soap in my eyes. Some aspects of this game were worryingly realistic, because the soap felt like it actually stung. I wiped it off with the back of my hand.

I imagined a huge wave roaring back at her. The three of us were amazed by the wave of water that hit the ceiling and splashed all of us. There wasn't a ton of room in the tub. I didn't even know if that amount of water was even in the tub. I guessed that the laws of physics didn't exactly apply inside of a game where I could disappear and reappear in a cloud of red smoke. Obvious to everyone but me, probably.

"What the fuck was that?" I asked. But the two girls acted like it was totally normal to see a huge wave coming from the garden tub and continued to splash each other with water. I was watching the motion of their tits as they giggled and tried to dodge the water before coming back and splashing the other girl.

"Doesn't Bianca look hot like this, Felix?" Amber asked me.

Outside of the game, it would probably be what Neil Strauss called a shit test. But inside of the game, I felt comfortable saying, "Of course she does. She's always fine."

Bianca came over to trail a wet hand over my shoulder before pulling me in for a kiss. With my peripheral vision, I could see that Amber tapped both of our shoulders to get in on the action. But Bianca just gave Amber the cold shoulder, blocking her with her body.

"Hey, none of that," I scolded Bianca, breaking the kiss even though her hands were still on my ass. She'd been touching me like I was a god or made of pure gold. "You ladies have to share."

Amber pulled hard on my shoulder and crashed her mouth into mine. If she'd tried that in real life, our teeth would've collided in a painful way. But inside of the game, the memory or whatever it was of Amber had perfect control of the motion and slipped her tongue into my mouth in the way that she knew that I liked. I felt like she was attacking me, her hands all over my body. I understood that it was a power struggle between Amber and Bianca, like goddesses fighting over the Golden Apple of Discord. But I wasn't going to call them out. It was nice, after a lifetime of being mostly ignored, to be fought over by two hot chicks.

Amber's kiss went on and on. I could feel Bianca trying to get Amber's hands off of me and pull me back. But she couldn't do it. I could feel her pulling harder and harder, until she climbed out of the tub and tried to grab Amber's hair to pull her out of the tub.

"Holy shit!" I yelled. "Stop that, Bianca. You have to share me."

She gave me a pout but stopped. "I don't want to..."

"You bitch," Amber said, touching her scalp. "You tried to make me bald."

Bianca hissed at her. She didn't look beautiful anymore.

"Bianca, apologize."

She gave me a glare that could've killed. "I'm sorry."

"You didn't mean it," Amber commented.

"Fuck off," Bianca responded.

"Hey now," I said. Just a few minutes ago, I'd been marveling at my luck. Two hot girls fighting over me? Yes, please. But now it wasn't as fun, because Bianca was being weirdly possessive. It didn't even make sense, because Amber was my fiancée.

Then I remembered hitting Bianca with a dose of pheromones. My body felt cold all of a sudden. It had been awesome when she'd immediately decided to blow me, but maybe this was the dark side.

"Are you incapable of sharing me?" I asked Bianca. "Tell me the truth."

"She cheated on you, Master," Bianca spat. "She's not worthy."

"She cheated on me with you," I reminded Bianca. "You're not blameless."

"But I've made up for it. And I wasn't engaged to you," Bianca protested.

"That's true," I admitted.

"I'll make it up to you, too, Master," Amber interjected.

Bianca and I turned to her, surprised. "What do you mean?"

"I'll do anything to make it all up to you. And I won't have to call my mom and explain what happened."

"Never understimate Amber," I told Bianca. "Now, are you going to play nice, or do I need to send you away?"

The threat was enough to bring Bianca to her knees, tears in her eyes. "Please don't, Master. I can't live without you."

I never thought I'd be hearing those words from Bianca, even inside of a virtual reality simulation. Kneeling, I kissed her silky smooth dark hair. "I know." I put a hand under her chin to meet her eyes with mine. "Will you play nice from now on?"

"If you want to... if you want to fuck other women, Master, you can."

"I don't need your permission, Bianca."

She still looked heartbroken. I wished that I could fix things. As soon as I thought that, I saw a little pencil floating over Bianca's head. It looked like an editing button. What was this new button? I hit the button. Immediately, a dialogue box popped out.

———

Edit Bianca? YES or NO

I DIDN'T KNOW what it was, but I clicked YES. All of a sudden, I saw a bunch of traits, like her personality and her physical attributes. It looked like I could edit anything about her that I wanted. Immediately, I scrolled to her "jealousy" setting and set it negative 50. I didn't know what that did, but I could see a slider near the bottom of the screen going up to 100. Reading the label, I realized that I'd just turned Bianca into a voyeur. A vague remembrance of high school French class made me think that for a woman it might be "voyeuse." Either way, she was really into exhibitionism and watching other people get it on in public spaces, which I thought would be very fun to try out.

I flipped to her physical attributes. I wanted to give Bianca longer hair, longer than a certain dark-haired celebrity's hair, the better to pull it. But as soon as I touched the slider, it told me that I was out of editing points until the next level. Well, shit. It hadn't warned me that there were a finite number of changes I could make at one time. I could see that in the corner, I could buy in-game coins to enable me to make more changes, but I didn't need to make Bianca more attractive really. She was pretty fucking hot as it was. And if I waited, her hair would just grow out.

I wondered then if it would grow. These projections were based on my mental images. So couldn't I just imagine Bianca with longer hair? I closed my eyes and imagined Bianca's hair lengthening. I also regretted

ARTIE PFEIFFER

spending all my editing points on moving her jealousy to negative 50 and moving her voyeur stat up. I would've liked to do a few minute tweaks, just because I could. I wouldn't make that mistake again.

Opening my eyes, I couldn't tell if Bianca's hair had changed at all. I didn't think that it had. I guessed that I'd have to wait for a little while to modify Bianca or Amber or shell out real money for in-game coins.

"Is she okay?" Amber asked, touching my shoulder.

"Yeah." Bianca was motionless on the floor. Apparently the change was going to take some time for her to absorb. I pulled her into my arms and put her on the couch. I made a mental note to figure out how to clean stuff in the game.

"C'mere," I told Amber. I kissed her fore-head and nose before kissing her mouth. She gave me the kind of kiss that had played a big role in why I'd been with her. Right now, she felt like the woman with whom I expected to spend the rest of my life. "I have a question to ask you."

"Yeah?" Amber's voice was breathy after making out a little.

"Will you be my first Guardian?"

"What's that?"

"A warrior. You'll help me."

She backed away from me. "I don't un-derstand."

"Frankly, neither do I. But I'm trying to find a Guardian to take care of my castle. And if you don't want the job, I'll just wake Bianca up and we'll leave you alone."

"No!" Amber yelped. "I'll do it. I'll be your first Guardian."

Immediately, my screen was filled with red smoke.

"Kiss her, you asshole," Luci snarled in my ear. "Complete the binding."

I reached for her. Luckily, she hadn't moved much. I brought her mouth to mine and put my tongue inside of her mouth. As soon as I did, the red smoke disappeared. I moved my eyes as much as I could while I was kissing Amber, but I didn't see Luci anywhere. I didn't know if it was part of the tutorial, but she'd said that my tutorial was over. Maybe there was some kind of timely help system inside of the game. I made a mental note to tell the devs that they should make it so that you could recall whatever had already been said.

I saw that Amber's eyes had a red rim around the edges. The white part of her eyes was still white, but there was a subtle red ring around her iris.

"You feeling okay?" I remembered that when Bianca had been edited, it had taken her offline by making her sleep.

"I've never felt better," Amber murmured. I watched her slender hands glide all over her body. "Stronger, smarter, indefatigable..." She smiled up at me. "What do you command, Master?"

I knew what I wanted, but Luci would probably cockblock me if I tried to tarry too long here. "Come with me." I held out my hand. As soon as she took it, I imagined that we were back on my land.

"What the fuck!" Amber screamed. I guessed that she'd opened her eyes.

"There's a giant dog, Master! It's coming right at us!"

"Don't worry, it's just a hellhound. Temporary. Meet Amber, Rufus."

Rufus came and barreled into Amber, slobbering all over her.

"Ew!" she wailed, trying to push Rufus away.

She wasn't actually being hurt, so I let Rufus kiss her all over before I snapped my fingers and sent him back to his duties.

"Thanks for warning me about your guard dog," Amber bitched. Her normally perfect hair was all over the place and had dog slobber in it.

"It's not too late for me to replace you with Bianca," I warned her. She shut her mouth, although I could tell she was still unhappy.

"I can clean you up," I offered.

"That'd be much appreciated," she replied.

With a puff of red smoke, I made a bathtub appear with warm water inside. With another snap of my fingers, I had a naked Amber inside of it.

"Enjoy yourself," I told her before walking off.

"Wait!" she said. I turned around. "Aren't you gonna... you know?"

"I have duties," I told her. "I'm the Laird here."

"Why do you suddenly have an accent?" Amber inquired.

"No, Laird is my title. I'll have a chat with you about what you need to do in order to keep things going here, but it'll wait. I'm going to check on how things are going."

"Does that include that giant hellhound?"

"Yes." I turned and walked off. I could hear her splashing a little in the bathtub I'd conjured. I looked at my hands. In my domain, it seemed that I could do anything I dreamed, pretty literally. I snapped my fingers and had a spoon in my hand. I bent it with my mind and smiled down at it. It was good to be king.

I wasn't a king of course. I was a Laird at the moment. I didn't know how the game progressed. If I were in the real world, I'd be reaching for Wikipedia now. I'd seen a comic by XKCD which mocked

the Millennial inability to really remember basic facts about the world because a free encyclopedia was so readily
available. There was some truth to it,
though, because I definitely didn't understand any peerage systems. Maybe
that was a byproduct of being an American. Maybe I should give the designers
the feedback that a clear roadmap of
levels would be appreciated by the
American audience.

I kept walking until I reached the door of
my home. It wasn't particularly impressive. I wondered why I hadn't been able
to see it when Amber and I appeared
here. I put my hand on the knob, which
felt warm. Inside, my hellhound was
running in circles, chasing his own tail.

"Hey boy," I said, letting Rufus put his
paws on my shoulders and lick me. I
didn't like his breath, but I went and

looked him in the eyes. I could see various stats showing up on my screen.

"So Luci came by, Rufus?"

"Woof!" Rufus confirmed. He let go of my shoulders before running through a door. I followed him through and saw another version of all my screens and stats there.

"So there's a command center?"

"Woof!"

Rufus wasn't exactly the best conversationalist, but I had to admit that he was short and to the point. I sat down in a wooden chair in the center of the room. There were no controls. I wondered why there wasn't a keyboard or mouse until I realized that I was wearing all the gear I needed in order to interact with my command center already. Duh. I reached out

with my hand to scroll through the re-
ports of various disturbances, which
seemed to be of the minor demon
variety.

"Hang on, what's this?" There was an
intrusion that said that it was the celes-
tial variety. I double-clicked it with my
hand. More information spilled out. My
domain had been visited by an angel. It
was kind of cool, but I instinctively knew
that I was on the demon side from the
red smoke that kept showing up.

ANGEL VS. DEMON

"So what was an angel doing here?" I asked Rufus. In a cloud of red smoke, Luci appeared.

"Heya, big boy," she cooed, winking. I could feel my shoulders going back as I puffed up my chest. Rufus ran to her and she cooed at him, "There's my big boy." My shoulders immediately slumped. She had obviously been talking to the dog, not me.

"So you've figured out that you're on the demon side, huh?"

"How the fuck do you know that?" I'd been taught not to swear around women, but I figured those rules didn't apply inside of the game. Plus college had taught me that swearing was not a male-only privilege.

"Magic," Luci giggled. "You have on a helmet, remember?"

"Right." I'd been taking a bunch of mental notes. I felt my cheeks getting hot when I thought about all the times I'd checked out Luci's smoking body.

"Relax, I find it flattering."

If it were possible for my cheeks to get extra-hot, they were doing it now. Kill me now.

"Nah, I'll keep you around for a while." She threw her hair over her shoulder and told Rufus, "Run and play now."

Rufus hightailed it out the door. Luci jumped up so that she was sitting on a table that had just appeared in time. "Now you're wondering why an angel swung by your domain."

"Uh yeah." She was pressing her tits together with her arms crossed and I was trying really hard not to stare at her cleavage, but she was at the perfect height for it. I wondered if she had done it deliberately. Knowing Luci, she probably had.

"So Luci is short for Lucifer and I'm the Bad Guy."

"What? You don't look like a guy."

Luci smirked at me and snapped her fingers. Then she had horns, a tail, and a male body.

"What the fuck?" I screamed as I fell out of my chair.

"Calm the fuck down," Lucifer growled at me. "You stupid humans have anthropomorphized angels and demons who don't have reproductive organs. We don't need them. We can have them if we decide we want them, like when we're impregnating mortal women."

I was gaping at Lucifer in horror. I was attracted to a man? What the fuck was going on here? I got back into my chair.

"I'm not a man or woman, doofus." Lucifer rolled his eyes and snapped his fingers again. Luci was back, clad in a see-through lingerie teddy with lace everywhere that didn't conceal the dusky pink of her nipples. My tongue was about to fall out of my mouth, but I held it back in and swallowed really hard. "You're Lucifer and Luci in one?"

"Now you understand." Luci sauntered over to me, sky-high stilettos on her feet. She sat down in my lap. Even though Lucifer had just been there, I could feel myself getting hard as I smelled her delicate perfume. She stroked my cheek with the back of her index finger. "So you're in Hell or a version of it anyway. I'm the head of things here." She kissed my ear, which made my erection painfully hard.

"It feels like Hell," I said. I was really hard for her, but I also was horrified by the fact that she was an immortal being without gender.

"You have powers while you're here." She snapped her fingers and made a glass of cold lemonade. "Wanna drink?"

I took the lemonade from her slender hand and drained it. "Is it hot in here or is it just you?" It sounded like a pick-up line, but she was actually burning hot. I could feel warmth coming off of her in waves. My forehead was sweaty.

Luci slid off of my lap and dropped a burning kiss on my forehead. "You'll get used to it. It's hot as Hell in here." With a cloud of red smoke, she was gone.

I still had questions. Was the incursion by an angel part of some kind of Eternal War? Was I supposed to help the Hell side win? I wasn't bound by the morals I'd learned during my PRE classes on Sundays. If the game had me on the side of the demons, I was cool with it. Bad guys had a lot more fun than people who had to play by the rules. I stood up and stretched. If an angel had visited my domain, there was no real harm done. I asked Rufus to come back with an ear-piecing whistle that I'd learned from my baseball coach when I was still in Little League.

Rufus came running in, knocking over my chair in his eagerness to jump on top of me. I looked in his eyes and saw that he'd decided to join Amber in her bath. He was not the kind of dog who was afraid of bathtime. I also saw that Amber had totally freaked out and run for her life.

"You called?" A naked and dripping wet Amber came through the door. "That dog!" she screeched. "Do you know what he did to me?"

"Yeah," I said, having watched it play in the dog's eyes. "I do."

"Get rid of him!" Amber commanded.

"Babe, let's get this one thing straight: I'm in charge here." I saw her shoulders droop. "You're my First Guardian, which means something, but I'm not someone you can just push around anymore. Is that clear?"

"Crystal," she said in a tiny voice.

"Rufus is on loan for the first three days here. There'll be two more days after this when he'll be around, but after that, you'll be in charge of all of our security. It's a good thing that you're in the command center now."

"Command center?" She no longer looked miserable.

"C'mere and I'll show you." I patted my lap. I didn't mind at all that she was wet, although I figured that I didn't want to get too wet, either. I snapped my fingers so I could wrap her in a giant fuzzy towel. I let my chin rest on her smooth shoulder.

"So you can see all of the feeds from here and see if there's any trouble."

"But how do you use it? There aren't any peripherals connected to the screen."

I realized then that Amber apparently did not have the same abilities that I did. But of course I could wish them into existence. With a snap of my fingers, I made a floating mouse and keyboard appear. They didn't have wires and weren't supported by any kind of table.

"Wow!" Amber gasped.

"You're impressed that I made a key-board appear but you weren't startled by showing up in Hell?"

"Is that where we are? Hell?"

"Yup. You like the new digs?" I motioned with my hands. "It's not much, but it's home."

"I think it needs a woman's touch."

I groaned, remembering that every time that she said that, I ended up spending way more than I wanted to on interior decorating or whatever she wanted.

"Well, babe, just describe what you want and I'll give it to you. On one condition."

"Name it."

"Anal."

She gaped at me like a goldfish. "What?"

"I'd been too shy to ask you for it before now, but that changes today. You give me unlimited access to your tight little ass and give it up whenever I want it, and you have yourself a deal."

"Fuck no," Amber said, scrambling off my lap and clutching the towel around her. "That's my husband hole."

I let those words settle between us. "And I would've had it on our wedding night before you cheated on me with Bianca and who knows how many randoms. Anal or no deal."

"Fine," she snarled. "But I won't enjoy it."

"We'll see about that." I snapped my fingers and had a bottle of lube in my hand. "Bend over."

"What, now? Here?"

"Yup. Here. Now. Downward dog." I was never as thankful for Amber's dedication to yoga as I was right then. I could see her pussy and her asshole from where I was sitting. I squirted some lube inside of her.

"It's cold!" she yelped. I snapped my fingers. "Ahh!" she screamed because the lube was now squirting even deeper inside of her body. I could feel my body responding to the sight of Amber bent over with plenty of lube in her asshole. I took some of the lube and spread it on my cock. I'd have to see if I could edit Amber's ass once I got more points on the next level.

I slid the tip into her body. She'd never let me fuck her ass when we were engaged. Now that we weren't, she was bending over in front of me. But I had to remember that it wasn't real life. In real life, she'd never agree to this. That thought made me push my way in, my hands on her hips as she kind of tried to squirm away.

"It feels so..." she said.

"So what?"

"Tight... pressure." She was panting hard. My hands were merciless on her hips, gripping her hard enough to leave bruises.

"Breathe out," I told her. "Relax." I felt her muscle relax just a hair, and then I rammed inside of her. She screamed in front of me. If I hadn't been holding her up, she would've fallen to the ground.

"So... full." She was clenching her ass muscles around my dick. It was the first time that I'd ever been inside of any woman like this, and I had to say, it was new. It wasn't better or worse than pussy. It just felt like a tunnel with a door at the front of it. I'd pushed past her sphincter with a generous application of lube. And now that I was in her ass, I knew that I'd want this feeling all the time. Good thing that I'd already negotiated for it.

"Tell me what interior things you want."

She breathlessly rattled off a list of things she wanted. I didn't understand all of it, but I visualized what she was describing while I was deep in her ass and made it happen. I could hear her gasp of surprise and pleasure.

"Thanks," she said.

That was the moment that I stopped being any kind of gentleman and started jackhammering her ass. I kept her body in place like a blow-up doll made for my pleasure. She was letting out these little cries of pleasure-pain while I felt myself getting ready to shoot. And then I was ready to shoot and filled her ass with my come. Panting, I let go of her hips. Amber collapsed on the ground, too dazed to stand or do anything but stay right where she was.

"Holy shit," Amber said. I could see the marks on her hips where I'd held her. I could see her hand sliding down to touch her clit. "That was so hot," she moaned. "I love it when you take control in the bedroom."

If anything could convince me that I was inside of a virtual world, it was that. I didn't know if I'd call Amber a fem-domme, but I definitely followed her lead whenever she decided that we would have sex. I wondered why I didn't get to give her a hero's welcome when she came home from her business trips, but it made sense that she'd had little to no interest in fucking me if she'd spent the entire business trip fucking other people. I felt a little satisfied seeing my semen dripping out of her ass, the ass that she'd deprived me of for far too long. I wondered what our married life would've been like if I hadn't discovered her cheating in our bed with Bianca. She probably would've kept me pussy-whipped for the rest of our lives. It would've been hell on earth. I'd really dodged a bullet. And now Amber was at my mercy in a virtual version of hell, with a helpful version of Lucifer hanging around whenever I had questions. Life could be worse.

I snapped my fingers and made a shower appear. Levitating Amber, I spun her so that she was sprayed with soapy water from all angles before being rinsed off. I applied hot air, like she was a car going through a car wash, and she had big, fluffy hair when I was done. She was still naked. She still hard marks that would turn into bruises. Snapping my fingers, I made sure she was dressed in the kind of lingerie she normally refused to wear because she said that lace lingerie was too scratchy and that thongs went up her butt. But in my new reality, she said, "This is so comfortable."

I smiled to myself. This version of Amber was a lot nicer than the real world version. Suddenly, I felt my stomach gurgle. How long had it been since I had eaten anything? I'd eaten a cookie baked by Bianca inside of the game, but I needed to pause the game and grab something to eat.

I hunted for any kind of settings gear or log out button. There didn't seem to be one. I started to panic. If I logged out without saving, I'd lose all the progress. I didn't know if I'd have to convince Amber to be a Guardian again, but it hadn't been easy the first time. I could fuck everything up by closing it down.

There didn't seem to be a mechanism TO close it down, either. There was no power button. Was I stuck in this game until I got too sleepy or hungry to continue?

TRAPPED

$\mathcal{I}$ started to hyperventilate. What was going on with this game? Either the developers had designed a cruel system where you could only progress in the game if you could go without food or sleep... or something else was going on.

"Lucifer!" I shouted. "I want a word with you."

In a cloud of red smoke, Luci appeared. "I was getting some beauty sleep," she yawned, covering her mouth with a dainty hand with red-tipped nails. If I looked more closely. they kind of seemed like claws.

"Do you need to sleep?"

"No, but it's fun." She snapped the strap of her flimsy see-through nightgown that kind of looked like lingerie. It was in that weird space between a nightgown that girls actually slept in and something that was meant to be taken off. "You called?"

"How do I log out? How do I hit save? When do I get to eat?"

She put out her hand to stop me. When she touched my shoulder, I got an instant erection. I felt hard enough to drill wood. "One question at a time." She snapped her fingers and got a chaise longue to sit on. "Okay, so you're in a long-term program."

"A what?"

"It was in the papers you signed," she told me, rolling her eyes. "You're hooked up to stuff so that you don't need to eat or sleep. Those needs are taken care of. You're in a coma."

"I'm in a what!" I shouted.

"A coma," she continued patiently. "That's why you can stay in here for as long as you want."

I looked around. "But that's trapping me inside. When will you let me out?"

She giggled a little tinkly laugh that matched her body and not her terrifying demon form as a dude. "When you win the game, silly."

"How do I do that?"

"You have to go through all the levels and fight the Big Boss." She ran her hands through her long blonde hair. "Now if you excuse me, I was sleeping."

"But..."

She was already gone. Fuck. I didn't know how the Big Boss was. Did it mean I had to fuck her? It definitely sounded like good news if I got to fuck Luci. I looked at my erection and wished myself back to where Amber was.

She'd made her way to my bedroom inside of the castle. She was literally staring at her hands. As soon as I walked in the room, she turned and asked, "Do you think I have man hands?"

"No," I said immediately. I was dumb sometimes, but I knew better than to ever criticize her body.

"There was a blonde girl who came through and said I had man hands."

"You don't." I had an inkling who the blonde girl was. Couldn't Lucifer leave me alone? Apparently not.

"Well, I wanted to make sure. What do you do around her for fun, anyway? I'm bored."

"We can fix that," I told her. "I should show you the ropes."

The rest of the day was spent walking Amber through all the aspects of the domain. As long as she kept the heart of my lands safe, we would be okay. I didn't want to explain in detail what would happen if the caput fell. I just said that it would be bad.

"What's that?" Amber asked as we made

our way back to the command center. One of the screens was blinking red.

"Gotcha!" I said, looking at the list of incursions. "Let's go, Rufus!"

With a bark, Rufus ran in front of me to chase the intruder away. When we got there, though, nothing was there.

"Must've been a glitch," I said to Rufus. "I'll race you back to the castle." It felt good to stretch my legs. But Rufus was barking at some bushes right outside of my domain.

Were these the people who'd tripped my sensors? I saw some rustling in the bushes.

"I should warn you, I have a hellhound," I called out. "If you're helpless little bunnies, you're about to be slain."

"Fuck you, asshole," I heard coming from the bush. Out popped my waitress, the girl named Evelynn.

"Damn," I said. She was dressed in a tied off button-up blouse that pushed up her tits with most of the buttons undone and her midriff bare. I could see that she had a piercing in her belly button that winked every time that the light caught it. Her skirt was the size of a wide belt and revealed long legs.

"What are you doing here?" I asked Evelynn, confused. Sure, she was part of my life, but she wasn't as big of a part of it as Amber or Bianca.

"I heard that you could grant wishes," she replied.

"I'm not a fucking genie if that's what you think," I warned her. "Don't expect miracles."

"Listen, dickwad," she started, "I need the money to finish my PhD."

"In what?"

"Psychology."

I barely held back from rolling my eyes. My cousin had a PsyD, not a PhD, and she lived a terrible life working for what I called an insane asylum and what she called an institutional facility. "So you want to be a shrink."

She hissed at me, kind of like a cat. I took a step back. "It's not that simple."

I was pretty sure it was, but I let it go. "Anybody else there?" I asked when the bush kept moving even when Evelynn was out.

When she came out, I was pretty sure my tongue was on the ground like a cartoon character. She was dressed kind of like Evelynn was. If you'd asked me, they kind of looked like sisters. Faelyn had flowing black hair and a pointed chin, but their eyes were kind of the same. I kept staring at Faelyn's legs. She was wearing a skirt approximately the size of Evelynn's, except she was also wearing thigh-high socks that ended about an inch below the hem of her micromini or whatever the fuck those things were called. That tantalizing inch made her look more alluring than Evelynn, even though their skirts were the same length. It was weird that Faelyn was showing less skin but seemed more naked. It was the tease of seeing that one inch of skin, I decided. Faelyn was the kind of girl who would lead a guy on and tantalize him until she had him wrapped around her finger, not unlike Amber.

"I've been looking for an angel," I said.

"What kind of damned stupid pick up line is that?" Evelynn asked. "So can you take care of my college tuition or what?"

"I can, but you have to swear yourself to me and become a Guardian."

"I'm not swearing shit!" Evelynn said.

"So you want something for nothing, is that it?" I asked her. She looked at her shoes. "You think you can come here and just demand what you want? Fuck that. I'm done with being trampled on by bitches."

"I'm not demanding anything," Faelyn said, her voice soft. She extended a hand to me but ran into an invisible fence around the edge of my domain. "I was just attracted by the amount of magic you've been doing in here. I'm sure someone like you has a lot to teach me."

Looking more closely at her, I could see that Faelyn was dressed as a slutty schoolgirl. You know the type, the kind of schoolgirl that had to be spanked during detention or comes to a teacher begging for extra credit and promising anything in return. "Swear yourself to me, become one of my Guardians, and I'll let you in."

"I swear to become one of your Guardians in exchange for my wish," she rattled off quickly. I didn't know what her wish was. I guessed that it was just to take a look around. I touched the outside fence and told it silently to let Faelyn in. She crossed the barrier and knelt at my feet. "I pledge my fealty to you, Laird."

How did she know my title? I barely knew my title. I touched her head and said, "I accept your fealty. Go to Amber. She'll show you the ropes."

She literally licked my hand. I could see her eyes change colors for just a second. It looked like she had blue fire in her eyes. But in another second, it was gone. She had eyes the color of a cloudless sky, but they didn't have blue flames in there. She darted away, reminding me of a Youtube video I'd see once of a fox entering a chicken coop and going to town on the defenseless idiots there. I shook my head. Faelyn wasn't a fox among chickens. She'd sworn fealty to me, after all. Amber would take her in hand. Amber's status as my First Guardian meant something, right?

I talked to Evelynn next. "So you just

want to make sure that you have college tuition?"

"You think I want to wait tables for the next few years? All of the customers are shitty human beings."

"But you're planning on leaving at some point, right?"

"How many years do you want me to serve you?"

I felt like Evelynn had a better grasp of what was going on than I did. I didn't understand all of my powers or why my wishes came true in Hell. "Three years," I thought. I thought about making it three years and three days like in the fantasy books I'd read growing up, but three years would be enough.

"Done." She reached out to me, her hand extended for a handshake to seal the deal. For some reason, I accepted her differently than I'd received the other girls.

"Turn around," I told her.

I could see the confusion flicker across her face, making her furrow her eyebrows. But she turned around. I laid a quick swat on her right ass cheek. As she yelped in pain and surprise, she spun. I could see that her face had turned red from embarrassment and from anger.

"You!"

"You swore yourself to me for the next three years. If you can't handle a little love pat on the ass, how do you think you'll survive the next few years? Why don't I just keep you chained up?" I snapped my fingers and she was trussed up like a BDSM fantasy, the hardcore kind that I only watched sometimes. She had a ball gag in her mouth, but it was the kind that let air through. It was a little extreme for my tastes, but she looked good in black leather with chains wound around her slender body and binding her wrists and ankles so that she was at the mercy of her master. "Why shouldn't you spend the next three years chained to my bed, used when I feel like it?"

She shivered. I could see that her nipples had gotten hard, just thinking about it. With another snap of my fingers, we'd translocated inside of my castle. I barred the door so nobody, including Amber, could get in.

I knew that I could simply snap my fingers and take Evelynn's slutty clothing off, but I wanted to do it myself. "Stay very still," I commanded her. Then I made a slender but very sharp filleting knife appear in my hand. I could hear her intake of breath even through the ball gag in her mouth. She stilled as much as she could. I made the chains disappear from everywhere but her wrists and ankles, which connected her to the bed.

First, I was cutting off her skirt. I slipped the knife under the waistband and sliced through the fabric. Then I cut through her shirt, letting the tatters fall to the side. I cut through the center of her bra, which was pink lace. Then I cut either side of her matching pink lace thong and peeled it off of her. I held it to my nose. I could smell her arousal.

"Smell how much you want this?" I asked, putting it under her nose. She made a muffled sound behind the ball gag. I sank first one finger and then another finger inside of her. "You're wetter than an ocean." I licked her juices off of my hand. I didn't know if it was the decision of the developers or what, but she tasted like peach ice cream, better than most of the girls I'd gone down on, including Amber.

Another snap of my fingers had a bullet vibrator show up in my hand. I pushed it inside of her, getting it nice and wet. Her hips were writhing below me. She was making eye contact with me when she could, but I could see her face morph as she panted her way through an orgasm that she couldn't stop. I felt powerful with a girl beneath me, helpless to stop climaxing as much as I wanted. I was almost tempted to leave the bullet vibrator inside of her, but I didn't. I had other plans for it. I pulled it out of her. She'd coated it so thoroughly that there was barely any resistance.

"Relax," I commanded Evelynn. Then I began to penetrate her ass. I'd noticed it before, of course, while she was bending over in the restaurant. She looked great as her eyes showed some level of panic while the vibrator sank into her inch by inch. I could hear something like a scream trapped in her throat. "Let it in," I told her. I saw her nostrils flare as her sphincter loosened and let me in. When it was fully inside of her, and I let it sit there. With another snap of my fingers, I had a clitoral vibrator. It kind of looked like a butterfly. I imagined it glued to her clit. She jolted as I turned it up to the highest setting. I could see sweat pouring out of her body, collecting between her perfect tits. I licked her tits, sucking them into my mouth, and leaving bite marks on them. I admired my handiwork before I moved to her pale neck. I was going to mark it up with hickeys the way I always wanted to mark up my high school girlfriend Hailey's neck before she'd cheated on me and we'd broken up.

She squirmed as I bit her neck, breathing hard through her nose. I felt between her velvet-soft thighs before I found her core and slid my fingers back inside of her while my mouth was on her neck. I didn't know if she'd ever stopped orgasming at this point. I curled my fingers to attack her g-spot like it was an enemy laird's fortress. She was turning an alarming shade of red at this point. I thought about taking off the gag, but she couldn't suffocate to death inside of the game. Yeah, it was supposed to be Hell, but I doubted you could market a game where you fucked girls to death and have it slide by the censors or whatever authority rated games for the American market. So I relaxed and pulled back from her body. I noted with satisfaction that she was so wet from everything I'd done to her that there was a wet spot on the bedsheet under her pussy. Her eyes were closed as she went through mind-melting orgasms, one after another. She began to whimper behind her gag, and her eyes pleaded me to stop the sensual torment.

I didn't. "I could just leave you like this for three years, you know." In Hell and in my domain, I could make it so that anybody staying inside of my caput didn't need food. I could also make it so that she did need food and just keep fragrant food next to the bed that she was tied to. I was a bastard, but I didn't know how far I'd get.

I kind of felt hungry after going to town on her. I hadn't ridden her yet, but there was no rush. I had Amber, who'd been my sexual partner for a long time, and Faelyn. Why spoil things with Evelynn? I'd only ride her for the very first time once. I snapped my finger and made a perfectly cooked filet mignon appear on a table beside her with a side of real mashed potatoes, none of that powdered stuff, and steamed asparagus. I didn't even like asparagus that much, but it was what went with filet mignon in my head.

"Smells good, doesn't it?"

Not even a tiny whimper came from Evelynn. I admired my work. She had bite marks all over her. She was sweaty. She could move beyond arching her back as orgasm after orgasm hit her. Was it evil to hit Evelynn with so many orgasms? Could it have long-term consequences? I decided to leave her there for a while. I cut my steak and ate it as I watched Evelynn grow slowly more exhausted by being stimulated to climax an uncountable number of times. Maybe I could consider her body like performance art and just keep it on display in the castle. Of course I'd need to wish another bed into existence or move into another bedroom, but I'd figure out a way to make things happen. When I was done eating, I snapped my fingers again. Everything was gone. I could definitely get used to this.

"Have fun," I said in an absentminded tone to Evelynn as I left her alone and locked the door behind me. I could hear a low moan, but she was still gagged. I went to find Amber, who had Faelynn tucked into her lap as she showed her how to navigate the security feeds. Amber's hand was on a mouse that was using the top of Faelynn's thigh as a trackpad. Faelynn was wearing fio dental, a microkini that was a handful of string and scraps of cloth smaller than my palm. Smaller than half my palm. "Hello ladies," I said, summoning a chair and sitting down in it. "This looks cozy."

"Amber has been really nice," Faelynn said. Her voice was kind of high. "She's been showing me... everything."

Looking at Amber's other hand resting on Faelynn's opposite thigh, I got the idea that they'd gotten really close very quickly. "Good." I licked my lips, thinking about what we could do in a moment.

"Did you find the angel that wanted to get into your domain?" Amber asked lazily, although I was watching her hand inch higher on the inside of Faelynn's thigh. In another second, she'd begin stroking Faelynn's snatch.

"Uh, no," I said. "I just found Faelynn and Evelynn in the bushes."

"Where's Evelynn then?" Amber asked, but Faelyn was moaning on her lap now and I didn't think she was really paying much attention.

"I left her in the bedroom, chained to the bedposts with two vibrators attached to her."

"Is she going to stay there?"

"No," I decided in that moment. I might as well display her if she'd be performance art or whatever. With a snap of my fingers, I moved the bed that Evelynn was chained to into a glass cage that would be suspended over the main castle entrance, so everyone could see Evelynn the Ever-Orgasmic. I made sure that she had no other needs than being absolutely insatiable. A normal human woman would pass out after too many orgasms, so I had to modify Evelynn to handle what I required of her. At some point, I'd gotten more and never noticed it. Maybe it was because Evelynn and Faelyn had been so distracting. I had a small number of points, and I used them to edit Evelynn into her new role. I couldn't use any on Faelyn or Amber yet, because I had to hold out for the next level and they were both close to perfect anyway.

I could see a damp spot on Faelyn's bikini bottoms as she arched her back and moaned as Amber moved her hand faster and faster. I didn't know fi there was a camera that could record what was going on right now, but I'd definitely like a replay. Faelyn's nipples were hard points. I shut Evelynn's profile and snapped my fingers. Amber, Faelyn, and I were now in the bedroom on a gargantuan bed the size of two California kings. I ripped Faelyn's bikini off. Amber was able to spare her clothing by getting out of it before I could rip her clothes off, too. I told Amber, "Hold her wrists."

Amber scrambled to obey, kneeling naked above Faelyn, her tits bouncing as Faelyn playfully resisted. I licked one of Faelyn's hard nipples, which made her whole body shudder. I could tell that she was about to orgasm. Pinching the other one, I settled my mouth between Faelyn's thighs and began to taste her cream.

There was an organic creamery near my house. I went there when I was willing to pay a premium for organic, hormone-free dairy products made by hand. The dairy products were better than mass-produced stuff you'd find on grocery store shelves. Faelyn tasted like the extra-rich, thick chocolate milk I bought every so often. I was grateful that the developers made all the girls taste so amazing inside of the game. Zero calorie chocolate milk? I could get into that.

Faelyn was trying to squeeze her thighs together, trying to get me out, but she was beyond words. I'd stop if she said no, of course, but I didn't think that she could talk right now. So I kept my tongue where it was as she went absolutely wild below me. Amber's eyes were dilated as she watched me go to town on the girl she was holding down. I'd be willing to bet $100 that she was wet right now. It was crazy because we'd never had a third person in our bed before Bianca, but I would be more than willing to add a third woman to menage in the real world. Amber and I were breaking up, of course, but maybe before I had her leave, I'd talk her into something.

With a scream, Faelyn's back arched all the way off of the bed, dislodging my head from its spot between her soft thighs. She settled down with her eyes closed.

"I think she fainted," Amber observed. She poked Faelyn's face, but Faelyn didn't say anything. Faelyn's breathing was even, though, so I left her there.

"Come on," I told Amber, motioning for her to crawl to open space next to Faelyn. I settled her into my lap, astride, so that her face was on the same level as mine. She was tall for a girl, but it was her favorite position so we could make out and fuck at the same time. Her hands cradled my face as I aligned our bodies and I slid inside of her.

I had proposed to Amber for a reason. She was a pain in the ass and apparently a cheater, but she knew me. She understood my body and my needs. And right now, while I was inside of her and she was biting my shoulder, I had a hard time remembering why cheating was so bad. She was a hot chick who had fun. Inside of this game, I also had the opportunity to fuck as many people as I wanted. Why was it so wrong? Maybe I'd make a rule that she could only fuck other women and that was it, but we could work something out. It was hot to watch her fuck other ladies in front of me.

Amber squeezed her eyes closed. She panted really hard right before she orgasmed, and I watched as she fell over the edge. She kind of used me as a sex toy, which I didn't mind, because right now she was one of mine, too. Both of us apparently liked to watch the other fuck extra people. As soon as she climaxed and I felt the aftershocks, I pushed her onto her back, put my fists down above her shoulders, and started to hammer the fuck out of her pussy. I didn't have the stamina to fuck so many women for this many hours in a real body, but in virtual reality and whatever coma they'd induced, I could go for days, I felt. She was crying out beneath me, her hands trying to touch my back as I rocked the bed so hard that the headboard kept thudding against the wall. Faelyn was awake now, watching us on her side. Her long black hair was everywhere and she still was naked. Her hand was between her legs, slowly pleasuring herself while she watched me ram Amber like there was no tomorrow. She met my eyes and smiled.

I had to close my eyes then, because I could feel myself starting to spurt. And then I was pouring myself into Amber. It felt like gallons were coming out of me, although a real human body didn't have that much capacity. But it wasn't stopping. I wondered if it was like the wishes I had made for beds and stuff, because it seemed that I could climax for as long as I wanted. When I decided I wanted to get off of Amber, my cock stopped. I pulled out of her and snapped my finger. Faelyn and Amber showed up in a bathroom that I had just created with a thought. Like the bathroom I'd had in my apartment, it had an area big enough for the three of us to play together. I could see that Faelyn was ready for another round.

"Clean the First Guardian," I said, throwing a soapy sponge at Faelyn. Amber sat down on a little seat inside of the big shower area. Faelyn began to soap her up on her knees.

"Stand up and bend over," I told Faelyn. She stood up and bent to take care of Amber. I could see that Faelyn was still wet. I eased my dick inside of her pussy, and all Faelyn did was gasp a little. Her muscles were so tight that it felt like she was a virgin or something. She grasped me so hard that there was barely room for me inside of her tight body. But the point wasn't for me to widen her pussy. I pulled out of her and tapped the head of my dick against an opening that was much smaller.

"I'm going to fuck your ass now, Faelyn."

Her only response was to widen her legs as she continued to wash Amber. She was a good harem member. I started guiding my cock inside of her tiny asshole. I was soaked in her juices and the shower was spraying warm water over all of us. It made it simple to get inside of her as long as I took it kind of slow. But eventually I was all the way in and Amber was smiling with her eyes closed. I yanked Faelyn into a standing position by grabbing her tits. The same action had made Amber pout for two days when I'd tried it in the bedroom. Faelyn was too short to stand while I had my dick up her ass. Instead of trying to fuck her at a bad angle or use editing points, I simply imagined a no-slip shower stool so that she could stand while I pounded her ass, which was heart-shaped. In real life, I'd be lucky if a girl like this even talked to me, let alone let me have anal. She was so beautiful that I'd probably be too stupid to say a word to her. I tossed her hair over one shoulder so I could actually see my dick while I thrust and withdrew. I was still gripping her tits, which were firm and perky. They weren't all that big, but they didn't need to be. Other members of my harem would have giant tits. Faelyn's tits fit her slender body, and that was what mattered. I could feel my balls drawing up right before I came inside of Faelyn. Even though I was in the shower, I felt like I had become part of a fireball. Good thing that the water was there to dry me off. The steam was probably from the water's heat, but it felt like it had stopped me from combusting into actual flames. I eased myself out of Faelyn and grabbed the soapy sponge to clean myself off. Faelyn was sitting next to Amber's exhausted body, smiling up at me, her long black hair wet. She kind of looked like a mermaid or a siren, one of those sexy enchantresses that lured sailors to their doom.

"Are you satisfied, Master?" she asked in her extra sweet voice.

"For now." I said, leaning down and kissing her mouth. "I want us to be dry." I thought of those Dyson handdryers that could get your hands clean in a few seconds without using paper products.

Immediately, the shower was full of a high wind that made everything go everywhere. My eyes stung from the hot wind around it and the soapy sponge hit the wall with a thunk before falling to the floor. I snapped my fingers to make it go away. As soon as I could open my eyes again, I saw that my skin felt dry and kind of cracked. I'd gotten it wrong, I understood. I would've done better if I had summoned fluffy towels.

Oh well. I snapped my fingers to bring us back into the bedroom. For some reason, my eyes felt like they were droopy. Maybe all the fucking inside of this game made my comatose body feel like it was actually having sex. I didn't understand why, but I curled up beneath the covers between the naked bodies of Amber, who was asleep, and Faelyn, who was not. I was on my side, with one arm resting on Amber's hip, while Faelyn's small body was curled against my back.

"Sweet dreams, Master," she whispered

into my ear the second before I fell asleep.

———

WHEN I WOKE UP, I had morning wood. I stretched out, expecting to see that Amber was on yet another business trip. But she was right there in front of me. I marveled again at my luck before I remembered what had happened. I wasn't going to marry her after all. Before I had time to be sad, though, a small hand came to grab my erection.

"What the fuck!" I yelped before remembering that I'd gone to bed with Faelyn, too. She caressed it, her hand gliding up and down. I closed my eyes because it felt so good. Her other hand started to caress my balls, tickling me a little bit but in a sexy way. I could feel pre-come coming out of the tip of my dick. She spread it all over, using it as lubricant for her hand to go a little faster.

My hips were moving of their own accord. Even though Faelyn looked like an innocent 19-year-old schoolgirl with her short skirt and high socks, she definitely knew what she was doing. Before I knew it, I was spraying my load all over Amber's sleeping body.

"Perfect," Faelyn said. Her tone was satisfied. She climbed half on top of me and bent to lick up all of my seed from Amber. She kind of reminded me of a cat licking up milk, but the way she moved was a little different. I had a naked woman draped over me, cleaning up my former fiancée with her tongue, though, so I wasn't complaining or kicking anybody out of bed. When she had cleaned Amber, Faelyn wiggled between our bodies. She slung one long leg over my hip, bringing my cock right next to the perfect spot. She started kissing my jaw and neck, her hand pinching my ass. "Why don't you give me some more, Master?"

As tempting as it might normally be to spend the day fucking Faelyn and Amber, I vaguely remembered that time was ticking. If I stayed in bed all day with my new acquisition and the First Guardian, I'd be wasting the time that I had with the protection of the hellhound. It was surely the second day, or was it the third? Time didn't move the same way here that it moved on Earth. I tapped my wrist to make a watch appear. I had 26 hours left with Rufus in my care.

I got out of bed immediately, regretting that I was leaving a warm bed with two naked women in it. But if I wanted to keep my caput and from it my domain, I needed to get moving. "Listen to Amber," I told Faelyn. "Fight off intruders and protect the domain." With a snap of my fingers, I made my way back into my apartment. It was weird to go there. I could still see the tray of cookies and Bianca was there, dressed in...

What was she wearing?

BIANCA

"*B*ianca?"

I was a little bit stunned by her transformation. I'd made her lack any kind of jealousy and turn into an exhibitionist. She was dressed like a stripper, but strippers at least started their sets with some kind of clothing on. Everything that Bianca was wearing was either sheer or just not there. She was wearing some kind of leather bikini that had the string parts but the scraps that normally covered her tits were gone. It was just an empty triangle.

"Do you like it, Master?" She was wearing a skirt about two inches long paired with thigh high black leather boots with stiletto heels. Her ass, which was curvy, was hanging out of a skirt that definitely could not cover it. The effect was that she looked more exposed than she would have looked if she was just outright naked.

In response, I pushed her over my kitchen table and pushed two fingers inside of her body. She was already wet for me. Thinking about how Faelyn had cleaned Amber up with her tongue made me snap my fingers to get a collar and leash on Bianca. Instead of pulling her hair, I kept a firm hand on a leash attached to a thick collar that was fastened around Bianca's neck. I pulled hard on it as I shoved myself inside of her willing body. Her breathing was labored and I didn't know if it was because I was choking her by pulling so hard or she was close to climaxing, but I pulled harder, until her upper body was bent into a C-shape. She was using her hands to brace herself on the edge of the table as I fucked her as hard as I could. "Touch yourself," I hissed into her ear. She was going to get bruises from how hard I was banging her against the table. Her hands left the edge and went to her clit. She was crying out now, maybe from pain, maybe from pleasure, probably from both. I was close to finishing when she screamed more loudly than before and shuddered in front of me. I used her body to finish before withdrawing. This time, I didn't bother with the whole showering thing. I just thought that both of us should be clean. I looked at her body critically. I could see the marks that would be bruises soon. While I enjoyed looking at a chick who had her tits out, there would be catfighting if I sent her back among the other Guardians. It'd have to wait for another day.

"Bianca, am I your Master?"

"Of course," she said, still breathless from the hard fucking I'd given her.

"Then go back to my domain and defend it. Play nicely with the other girls. And I'm changing your clothes." With a thought, I put her into a very short dress that covered slightly less than half of her tits and had a deep V in the front. The dress was so short I could see a lot of ass-cheek and could almost see her pussy. It looked hot. "I'll fuck you again later if you're very good."

She gave me a lascivious smile and took a single step towards me. I banished her to my domain with a wave of my hand. As much as I wanted to go for another round with a horny chick, I had other things to do. First, I had to get more Guardians. There weren't any actual quests past the First Guardian, and I wondered about it. But if other people were going to be attacking my domain, I needed to build up my defenses. I paced around my apartment. I had my general, my First Guardian. For all of Amber's faults, she was intelligent and knew how to handle people. Maybe a little too well in my case, but she could do the job. Bianca was a good follower. Faelyn didn't have a lot of talents beyond keeping her socks at the perfect height, but hey, maybe that ability would be useful at some point. Evelynn was useless except as a distraction. I knew that I'd be better off giving her a real job, but something about keeping her as a piece of performance art in a clear cage turned me on. It was irrational, but it was kind of like 24/7 porn and I didn't even have to worry about getting mysterious viruses on my computer. Evelynn the Ever-Orgasmic was fun to look at it, even if I never fucked her. I'd left her pussy open deliberately, just in case I wanted to engage in some public sex. Bianca would be into it, I was sure.

I kept thinking about more women to bring into the fold. My former next door neighbors might be a good start. They were dumb as rocks but I couldn't imagine any adult male not being distracted by them. While they disarmed and charmed any incoming enemies, Amber and the rest could kill off the invading forces. I smiled thinking about how surprised someone would be if they were confronted by topless twins and then summarily defeated. I'd be able to expand my land. But it all depended on my ability to convince more women to join me.

I guessed that my next stop should be to pick up the twins. With a snap of my fingers, I left my apartment.

CHEYENNE AND CECILIA

J was inside of their pool, which would be great in other circumstances. I was fully clothed at the bottom. I experimented to see if I could breathe underwater. I could not. I pushed off of the bottom of the pool to get to the surface and gasp.

"What are you doing here?" Cheyenne screamed. I'd surfaced right next to her giant flamingo tube. She was sipping on some kind of fruity adult beverage, which she immediately threw in my face as she tried to kick to the side.

"Cheyenne? You okay?" Cecilia came running from the kitchen, a meat tenderizer in her hand. As soon as she saw me, she hurled it at my face. I dodged and the meat tenderizer hit the surface of the water with a giant splash before sinking to the bottom. "Get out of there, you pervert."

I realized that Cheyenne was topless then. I normally would've noticed immediately. I'd gotten distracted by having a drink with alcohol get into my eyes when it was thrown in my face. Cheyenne's tits were pure perfection, I had to admit, although I was smug in the knowledge that Amber, my First Guardian, had bigger ones.

"Get out of here before I call the police!" Cecilia screamed at me. She was running back into the kitchen, probably to get a knife. I had to move fast.

"You want me here," I told Cheyenne.

"No I don't! Get away from me!" She was covering her boobs and looked like she was about to scream. I sighed before I pressed the button to release the hormones that had enslaved Bianca only a day ago.

Nothing happened. Cheyenne took in a big breath and was about to shout. I looked left and right before I pulled myself out of the pool, sat, and tried it again. I managed to do it a split second before Cheyenne yelled.

"What's that smell?" she asked instead, sniffing. "It smells like... the best..." Then

I saw her eyes flash red. "You." She paddled over to me and started touching my thighs. "You smell..."

"Chey?" I heard a little voice ask behind me. Cecilia had a knife in her hand. "What are you doing?" She frowned, dropped the knife on their patio table, and walked towards us. But as soon as she did, the pheromones hit her, too. "It smells... so good." She walked towards the two of us as if she were daydreaming. "I need..." I watched her hand go towards her cunt. Unlike Cheyenne, she wasn't topless and only wearing bikini bottoms. Cecilia was wearing a romper but was rubbing herself through it. "I..." Her eyes were glazed over as she literally started tearing the romper apart so that she could access what she needed. "I don't understand." But even as she said that, she put her head in my lap and sniffed me. I watched, bemused, as she started to yank the rest of the romper off of her. "This fabric is too rough. I can't..." I touched the shreds of the romper. The fabric was delicate, somewhat transparent, and soft as a feather. But Cecilia couldn't bear to wear any clothes anymore.

"Get away from him!" I heard Cheyenne say right before she slapped her twin on the back of her head.

"You bitch!" Cecilia retorted, finally tearing herself away from being nose deep in my crotch. I was about to see a catfight go down. Cheyenne succeeded in pulling Cecilia into the pool with her.

Fuck. I didn't have the editing points that I had used to modify Bianca's jealousy. I'd used the pheromones to save myself, but at what cost? Were the two of them going to drown each other? I already had tested my ability to breathe underwater in this game, and I clearly didn't have it. Maybe it would be a skill that I'd unlock later on. No matter what, I didn't know if I should dive into the pool and separate the girls or if they'd accidentally drown me by holding onto me and refusing to let me up.

They'd been down there long enough to make me worry. But as soon as I saw their heads break the surface, I sighed in relief. They were treading water and pulling each other's hair, just like they used to when we were tiny. Now that I was sure they weren't literally going to kill each other, I sat back and enjoyed the show. I'd break it up in three minutes, but as long as they did no lasting damage to one another, it was hot for two twins to fight over me.

"You slut!" Cecilia screamed at Cheyenne. "You have a boyfriend!

"So do you, slut-whore!" Cheyenne yelled back.

They were both professional cheer-leaders and part-time Instagram models. One of them cheered for our local bas-ketball team while the other cheered for our local football team. They each had a boyfriend who did the other sport, be-cause of the anti-fraternization policies in place. When Cheyenne tried to shove Cecilia against the metal rail attached to the steps, I stepped in and broke it up, plucking Cecilia out of the water. I was either much stronger in the game or Cecilia didn't weigh very much, because she felt like a pillow.

"GET AWAY FROM HIM!" Cheyenne screamed, jumping out of the water and trying to get Cecilia away from me.

"You stop that this instant," I commanded Cheyenne. She stayed still and started to cry.

"But!"

"No," I said, feeling like a preschool teacher. "You two can share. You're sisters, after all."

Cheyenne snorted, "No, we aren't."

"I think I'd fucking know, wouldn't I? I live next door to you guys, or I used to."

"We're both adopted," Cecilia said, shifting in my arms so that she could wrap her body around me like a koala and send a smirk over her shoulder at Cheyenne. "We're not really twins, we just look alike and were adopted by the same parents."

I was stunned by this information. We'd known each other for a long time, but nobody had ever told me. Even my mom, who probably knew, had never told me that their mom had never been pregnant. What the hell? "Okay, you're adopted sisters, and you should treat each other nicely."

I expected them to glare and complain some more, but Cheyenne said, "How nice?"

"Very nice," I responded. I let Cecilia drop to her feet and approach Cheyenne. Immediately, their lips locked. They'd been trying to drown each other only minutes ago! But as soon as I commanded them to be nice to one another, they'd obeyed me. I regretted wasting my editing points on Bianca when apparently it only took some commands. Now that I thought about it though, it might be different. When I had talked to Bianca, I had not completed the First Guardian quest. Maybe something was different now.

I could hear the sound of a lawnmower near us. In a few minutes, anybody who bothered to peek over the fence would get an eyeful. I tried to teleport us into the house with a snap of my fingers.

Nothing happened.

Why did some of my powers work and others didn't? To be fair, I'd used the pheromones on Bianca before, in the virtual version of the real world and not in Hell, so I knew that they worked, though apparently not underwater. I pulled them into the house physically. When I was holding Cecilia, she'd felt like a pillow. For some reason, while yanking them into the house, they had about the weight of a wheeled garbage bin, the kind that you keep outside. I could feel the weight, but it wasn't a lot. They were giving each other's tonsils a good check by the time I got them indoors. I pushed them onto a couch. I could see Cecilia tugging at Cheyenne's bikini bottoms and of course Cecilia had already torn off her romper. Cecilia's hand slid between Cheyenne's thighs with the ease of long practice and I had to wonder if they'd ever done this before. They lived in the same house, they were both hot, and maybe they had certain kinds of needs. I watched as Cecilia slid off of the couch and knelt next to Cheyenne before she started going to town on her. I tugged at the collar of my shirt. Cecilia was licking Cheyenne like an ice cream cone on an exceptionally hot day, like she wanted to catch every bit before it melted and made a mess on the table or couch in this instance.

"Master, you want to taste?" Cecilia turned and beckoned me forward. I imagined that she wanted me to go down on Cheyenne as well, but she ended up jumping on me, flinging her arms around my shoulders, and shoving her tongue inside of my mouth.

Cheyenne's juices tasted like melted ice cream. It was hard to pay attention to the exact flavor when Cecilia seemed to be determined to explore every part of my mouth. I wasn't sure if I liked it, but her legs were wrapped around me and she was grinding herself against my lower stomach and dick, so I couldn't complain too much.

Cheyenne evidently didn't want to be left out while Cecilia was making out with me. She also came off the couch, but I didn't notice until I realized she was ripping my own clothing off. I didn't know that she was strong enough to do that, but maybe something in the game made everything lighter than it usually was. In moments, I was also naked and she was positioning her sister at an angle so she could give me a handjob. In real life, I'd need lube to feel her soft hand gliding up and down my erection. Inside of the game, her hand had no trouble. I honestly didn't know if I could stand anymore. My knees felt like they were about to give out, so I moved Cecilia and myself to the couch, which hindered Cheyenne's access to my dick.

To accommodate her, I shifted so that I was prone with Cecilia on top of me. Cheyenne knelt, as Cecilia had done, to give me a blow job. The angle of Cecilia's body was different now and she started biting my ear and neck. I could feel the heat rising inside of me, and when Cheyenne tugged my cock at the exact right angle, I came all over her face and tits. I pushed Cecilia off of me so that I could see Cheyenne.

"So much come, Master," Cheyenne said, trailing her index finger through it and sucking it off. "Yum."

"I want some!" Cecilia screamed. I thought I'd fixed the jealousy, but maybe I'd just made them horny for each other. She began to lick Cheyenne's tits to suck up all of my come. Then she started licking Cheyenne's face to clean off all of my come. Cheyenne stroked Cecilia's back as Cecilia licked her. I watched as Cheyenne's hand slid down Cecilia's back, hip, and ass before going between her legs and sliding into her cunt. Cecilia gasped a little bit before she rocked against Cheyenne's hand. I could tell that she was orgasming on the spot. I knew my ability to snap myself around only worked in Hell or possibly just my domain, so I couldn't instantly move us from the living room into the bedroom. I also knew that their mom wouldn't be around, which helped. Their mom was a total MILF, no doubt about it, but I didn't know if a married woman would be as susceptible to pheromones or if I would need to try something else.

When Cecilia had cleaned off Cheyenne entirely, I walked over to the girls and told them, "We're going upstairs."

They pulled me with them as they ran up the stairs, one of the girls holding each of my hands. We must have sounded like a herd of stampeding elephants. Then they threw open the door to their shared bedroom.

I had to say, it looked like something from a porn set. Their shared bed was not a king sized bed. It looked like something you'd find in the Playboy Mansion, or maybe what people imagined existed in the Playboy Mansion.

"You girls have a lot of parties or what?" I asked.

"Or something," they giggled. I suspected they might have multiple players over after games. I wondered what their boyfriends thought of it and let that thought go. In the real world, I'd get my ass beaten for daring to even look at these girls naked. But here I was, in a bed that might be out of my own fantasies, and Cecilia was already straddling my body and pushing my shoulders down.

"I get to go first," she explained, "because Cheyenne got a faceload of your come first and we have to share equally." I wasn't a Snickers bar that had to be divided by one sibling while the other kid chose the piece that they wanted, but I also wasn't opposed to being shared between the two girls.

Cecilia's tits were bouncing as she rode me like she was on Secretariat and racing for the finish line. Her hair was wild, moving with her. She looked like a goddess or enchantress, fucking men at their own peril. I came within about a minute, but she wouldn't stop.

"Get off, it's my turn!" Cheyenne said, pushing Cecilia so that she fell off of me. Before I could protest, Cheyenne was on top of me. And for some reason, Cheyenne knew how to give a good show. She started sucking on her own fingers while fucking me. She was moving her body sinuously, like a snake, unlike the bunnyfucking that Cecilia had just given me. She was pinching and rolling her own nipples while moaning on top of me. I felt like I was on a porn set but I wasn't protesting. She started rubbing her clit while she moved up and down on me, and I could see the moment when she let go and gasped for air. Before she was even done, Cecilia pushed Cheyenne off of me and started sucking up all of our combined juices. I could go an unlimited number of times within this game, so I was still hard while she gave me my second blowjob in a very short amount of time. I came in her mouth, and came again, and again, and I felt like there was no limit. Inside of the game, my body wasn't constrained by the normal physical limitations. I hadn't had multiple orgasms before, although I'd tried, and I had to say that feeling the wave hit me over and over again made me feel like I was drowning in the most pleasant way imaginable. Cecilia couldn't swallow all of it, and it was sliding out of her mouth, dripping on my body, and onto the sheets. Cheyenne came to me and started making out with me and biting my neck and shoulders. Being double-teamed like this kind of felt overwhelming, but if I had any say, it would be happening again.

Eventually, Cecilia jumped on top of my dick again. She was facing away from me this time in reverse cowgirl as she took me in a slower rhythm than before. I was exhausted while Cheyenne moved away from making out with me and started kissing Cecilia while slapping her clit. I wondered dimly if they wanted to milk all the come out of me that they could. I could feel Cecilia's muscles tensing and fluttering around me while she came. I'd never stopped. I almost felt disassociated from my own body now. I could feel everything as they fucked me and each other, but a part of me was watching the show. I wished that I'd thought about filming us all fucking. Did recordings exist in this game?

Eventually, Cecilia rolled off of me, sated. Cheyenne had a look in her eye like she wanted to go another round, but I motioned for her to rest her head on my shoulder. I stroked her soft, long hair. It felt like silk beneath my fingers and trailed to the top of the curve of her ass. I slapped her butt, just because I could.

"Hey!" Cheyenne yelped. The bed was messy now, but I had other concerns. If I fell asleep here, I'd probably run into their mom. Under other circumstances, I'd just hit her with whatever chemicals I'd used on Bianca, Cheyenne, and Cecilia, but I would wait for a while. I couldn't teleport us anywhere but Hell. Back there, I had concerns and responsibilities. Topside or in the simulation of my real life, I was responsible for fucking Cheyenne and Cecilia as many times as I wanted.

"Cee?" I heard someone shout. Someone was banging on the door. It sounded like a battering ram. "Baby, I'm here to pick you up for lunch!"

"It's my boyfriend!" Cecilia yelped. She looked like she was looking around for clothes.

"I can get us out of this, if you both agree to come with me and do what I say."

They looked at each other. A moment of unspoken twin-like communication passed between them. "Yes," they chorused in unison. Then I snapped my fingers and we were in my bedroom in Hell.

Amber had done something with the place. Obviously I was the one who could wish things into existence, but she'd moved furniture and stuff around. It was nice, if unfinished.

"Where the hell are we?" Cheyenne asked, sounding like her old self.

"Hell," I replied, smirking. "We're working on my new digs."

Cecilia got off of the bed naked and roamed around my bedroom, checking things out. "It's a big room."

It was. Obviously it was as big as I wanted it to be. It would never work as a ballroom or anything, but surely the master of the castle should have his own space. I snapped my fingers and put a set of transparent lace lingerie on Cecilia's naked body. I appreciated the view, but I also loved ripping clothes off of her perfect body.

She put a hand on her lingerie. "This shade of pink is my favorite color. How did you know?"

I rolled my eyes. "We used to be best friends, remember?"

Cecilia smiled at me, a little misty-eyed. "Yeah, I remember."

Cheyenne put her had on my dick, which got my attention in a hurry. "What are we here for? Why are we in Hell?"

"We're here in my castle because it's where I can keep you safe. And you agreed to it, so you're Guardians now."

Another moment of wordless communication passed between them. I couldn't decide if I liked it or not. "What does that mean?" Cheyenne asked, her hand sliding up and down my cock. She was literally pumping me for information.

"It means that you're responsible for distracting any invaders." I was pretty fucking distracted myself. In this game, there was no limit to what my body could do. I was rock hard and ready to go again. "It's why I came to visit the two of you. No man could resist both of you."

Cheyenne smiled at me before she touched my balls in a way that made me explode. I came all over her hand, the semen falling to the sheets. "That was the right thing to say."

Cecilia asked me, "If we're in a castle, can I have a princess dress?"

"Which princess, sweetheart?" Since I could fulfill any wishes with an easy snap of my fingers, it was easy.

"Cinderella," she said. In a moment, she was wearing a slutty version of a ball gown. There was a shitload of fabric, but it was all transparent. I could see her tits easily. She twirled, spinning in circles and laughing. "This is fun!" The transparent and lightweight fabric flew around her.

"I want one, too! Make me a Sleeping Beauty dress." With a snap of my fingers, she was clothed in a closer cut ball gown. I liked Cheyenne's hair curled, so I snapped my fingers and gave her Sleeping Beauty curls.

"I want a tiara!" Cecilia demanded. With a snap of my fingers, I settled a diamond tiara on top of her head.

"I want a mirror!" Cheyenne said. I was getting tired of being a fucking genie, but I made a bunch of mirrors appear in my bedroom anyway. The entire ceiling was now a mirror, and it looked like a ballet studio now. Cheyenne and Cecilia ran to the mirrors and admired themselves. Their vanity was not unexpected, because they'd been beautiful for their whole lives. When they were with someone who could give them everything that they wanted, why shouldn't they demand the best? I decided that Cheyenne should get a small golden tiara. It had sapphires in it to match her dress or what little there was of it. She looked over her shoulder and gave me a giant smile when it appeared on her forehead.

I could tell myself that I was dressing them like this so that they would be the first line of defense, but I was kidding myself. Amber had demanded all I had to give, and these girls, given half a chance, would run over me. But in my domain, I was the Master and Laird. I poofed them to the gate.

"I wasn't done looking at myself," Cecilia screamed. I didn't know if the pheromones had worn off or they were just brattier than Bianca, but I was done with their shitty behavior.

"I'm spanking your ass," I warned Cecilia. In a second, I had her bent over and tied down on a spanking bench.

"Let me go!" Cecilia screamed again.

"You agreed to listen to me and do what I wanted before we came here. And you're being a giant brat." Flipping her skirt up, I let my hand fly. I admired the pinkness of her ass before landing another blow. And another. And I could see and smell that she was glistening between her legs and turned on, even if she was squirming on the spanking bench.

"Can I get a turn?" Cheyenne asked, her hand rubbing between her legs as she watched me spank Cecilia.

"Sure." I made an identical spanking bench appear and strapped Cheyenne to it. I also slid a small jeweled anal plug with a fluffy cat tail attached into Cecilia's pussy to get it wet before sliding it gently into her red ass.

"Ahh!" Cecilia cried out as I pushed it into her. She wasn't saying no, though. I spanked Cheyenne's ass to make it as red as Cecilia's. They looked great like this, dressed in transparent gowns with red asses, bent over for anyone who wanted to take them. There were other members of my harem who would play with them, but definitely any red-blooded male who came to my domain would not be able to resist them. I'd uncuff them if I decided it was good.

How would they amuse themselves without me? I thought about Evelynn the Ever-Orgasmic. I took pity on my neighbors and snapped my fingers to put giant Hitachi vibrators straight into their cunts, so that anytime I wanted to use them, they'd be ready to ride. I made sure that like Evelynn, they needed nothing else. I'd take pity on the more often than the woman I kept on display in a glass cage. I snapped my fingers to teleport myself up to where I'd decided to keep her.

I didn't think that she had the power of speech anymore. Her body shook as the orgasms rippled through her, one after another without end. She was only sworn to me for three years. What would three years of non-stop orgasms do to a woman inside of this game? How did time even pass? I'd gotten the hellhound for three days, and I didn't know why day it was in Hell. I tapped my wrist to make my watch show up. I had a few hours left with Rufus on guard. I sighed. He was a good dog, and I didn't think that my defenses were all that impressive. I imagined that other players were even more successful gathering women from their memories to guard their domains. I'd end up someone's vassal on Day 1.

Evelynn opened her eyes and saw me. She was moving her lips, but I couldn't hear her. I snapped my fingers to get myself inside of the glass cage.

"Please," she panted. I didn't know what she was asking for, but I stroked my cock. I probed her gently with the tip and her head fell back as she arched hard. With a snap of my fingers, I made the two vibrators disappear until the only thing touching Evelynn was my dick, which was sliding faster than someone would go on one of those giant water slides. She was impossibly tight, but of course I'd kept the vibes on her clit and in her ass, so her pussy was almost untouched by the experience. She clenched around me as she orgasmed, which felt fantastic. She was milking my seed out of me and couldn't stop orgasming. I knew I could keep my dick in her for a week and she'd still feel the same. There wasn't much value in Evelynn the Ever-Orgasmic in terms of my domain's defense, but she was still fun to have around.

With a sigh, I slid out of her and replaced the two vibes. With a snap of my fingers, I left her cage and went back into the security room, where Amber and Faelyn were rolling around the ground. Faelyn had straddled Amber and was tickling her with a feather.

"Girls!" My voice cracked like a whip. "Where did you even get the feather?"

They jumped to their feet looking sheepish. "I don't know, I just found it," Faelyn said.

"Amber, describe what you want for interior decorations." I listened while she listed a shitload of things that I'd never bother with. With a snap of my fingers, I put everything where she wanted it to be.

"Faelyn, you're coming with me."

Amber's eyes looked hard and angry, but I was the Laird. So she had to watch as I settled my hand on the curve of Faelyn's small waist and took her out of there. As soon as we had passed the door, I pushed Faelyn up against the wall. "Are you wet?" I whispered in her ear before sliding a hand under her short skirt and finding out for myself. She wasn't as wet as Evelynn had been, but she was ready. I snapped my fingers to put us on the roof of the castle. There was a lookout up here to watch my domain. There were cameras, of course, but I controlled them and I knew Amber might get off watching me fuck another girl.

"On your knees." Faelyn immediately sank to her knees. She was wearing her socks, which had to help.

"Open your mouth." Faelyn's jaw dropped obediently, like someone going to the dentist. I slid my dick into her small mouth and gripped her silky hair with my fingers. "Now blow me."

Faelyn might look like a schoolgirl, but the blowjob she gave me was a 10 out of 10. I had to snap my fingers and get a chair, because I would've fallen over. If she were someone I knew in real life, I'd wonder if she was some kind of prostitute who specialized in blowing guys for a living. She could have a PhD in sucking dick. I felt my muscles tighten right before I blew. She sucked it all down. The other girls couldn't handle the quantity of seed flooding their mouth, but Faelyn didn't let any of it escape. She get her mouth around my dick through too many orgasms to count before I pulled my dick out of her mouth and let her take some deep breaths.

"You could teach the other girls how to do that," I commented, still breathing hard.

"But then where would my advantage be, Master?" Faelyn inquired, tossing her hair over her shoulder. "I like being special."

"You'll always be special." I motioned for her to get into my lap. She curled herself around me, her head on one shoulder. I ran my fingers through her beautiful hair. "What was the wish that you wanted in exchange to becoming one of my Guardians?"

"It's a surprise," she giggled. "I want you to be surprised." She kissed me on the mouth then and thoroughly distracted me until I heard a bark coming from below.

RUFUS AND FIRST INCURSION

"*D*amn," I swore. I looked at my watch. Time was nearly out.

I snapped myself down to Rufus, who came barreling towards me. I read an apology in his eyes for not being able to stay longer. "It's okay, boy," I said, petting him gently. "You've been a good guard dog."

He licked my face one last time before bounding off. I could see that he had his own abilities, because he vanished in a puff of red smoke like so many things around here did. He had a way with wordless communication that made me miss having any male company. So far, I'd gotten a harem of chicks, which was awesome, don't get me wrong. And I'd spent way too many years of my life when the only places I went beside work and home were sausage parties. But I missed having male companionship.

I dug around and looked for another quest. I didn't understand why another one hadn't appeared yet. Rufus was gone, so the PvP...

Oh shit. My stomach sank. Rufus running home meant that my Guardians were the only line of defense between me and the other players who had started at the same time as me. As soon as they marshaled their forces, they'd be on my doorstop, trying to take my fortress and women. I wasn't about to let that happen. I snapped myself back to the security room. I set all of our sensors on the highest alert levels, so a leaf blown around by the breeze would trigger them. I didn't know if people had started at exactly the same time as me, but I wasn't going to let myself hang around like a bleeding fish darting in front of a Great White. I heard my middle school basketball coach tell me that the best defense was a good offense, but I shook my head. He was the dad of the bully of my nightmares. As a kid, I'd been petrified of Ricky, but as an adult, I wondered what kind of fucked up home life he'd had that made him take it out on his classmates. He'd eventually ended up in juvie and never came back to school after he torched his ex-girlfriend's car the day that she broke up with him.

I shook off this weird wave of sympathy for an asshole I tried not to remember. The lesson was beaten into me. I was not waiting for someone to knock on my door. I could be the one knocking on other people's doors. I didn't have the manpower or womanpower or whatever you wanted to call it to fully defend my caput and attack anybody else. I was going to have to make a choice: I could sit in my fortress like a scared little girl or I could go and extend my domain by capturing other players' caputs. I didn't have the womanpower I needed right now but that was a temporary problem because I could get some more.

"Amber," I called, snapping my fingers. She had whipped cream on one breast and appeared to be having fun. "I need you to seal my entire domain. Nobody gets in or out. If someone tries, you send for me."

"How?" she asked, licking whipped cream off of her lips.

I snapped my fingers again. "Use this pager."

We both looked at the pager. "Uh, why are you using a pager and not a cell phone?" she asked.

"Because there's different reception." It was bonkers, but for some reason I got the impression that cell phones didn't work in Hell. It didn't make that much sense because of course I could make anything work. I snapped my fingers and made the latest iPhone drop into my hand, fully charged. It was searching for a signal. I knew that I'd confirmed my hunch because I'd had a friend in high school who had a basement where we all hung out and all of our phone batteries were always dead when we were down there, because there was no signal to be found. I knew Hell was like that basement. But why did pagers work? A mystery I'd have to figure out later, if I even remembered. I snapped my fingers to create another pager and stared at the buttons.

I could barely even remember how to use a pager, but I snapped my fingers and transported myself Topside again. I ended up in Cheyenne and Cecilia's home. Their mother's car was in the driveway. "Cheyenne!" I heard a voice call. "I just bought some lunch for you. Come out while it's still hot."

I grinned and knocked on the door. "Hello."

She opened the door and looked at me. She had a slight grimace on her face. "Oh, it's you."

She was the same woman who used to feed me cookies and lemonade when I played with her adopted daughters. "Yes. And I know where your daughters are."

"Well, come on in," she huffed. "I have some lemonade around here, I guess." She went into the kitchen and took out a brightly decorated pitcher, the one that I remembered from back when I was actually welcome in this house. "Here you go."

She could be a little more gracious about it, but she was from Georgia and knew that she had to take care of guests. She put the pitcher back into the fridge in a move that I thought meant she didn't want me to stick around. "So where did they go? They've never just run off like this, and one of their boyfriends texted me that he was supposed to have lunch and my daughter wasn't around."

"I took them." I winced.

"What do you mean, you took them?"

"They didn't want to stay here, so they're at my place."

"Your place? Your crummy apartment in a bad part of town?"

My apartment was hardly in a bad part of town, but whatever. "No."

"Stop being cryptic and tell me where my children are."

"They aren't your children."

Her face went bone white. "What did you say?" she hissed.

"You adopted them."

"You asshole," she snarled, reaching for a frying pan. I viewed it with consternation, because I could still get hurt in the virtual version of my real life. "Tell me where my daughters are and then never darken my doorstep again."

I said, "If you promise to obey me, I can take you to them."

"No way in hell!" she screeched, coming for me with the frying pan. I snapped my fingers to get myself back into Hell. Then I snapped my fingers to reappear in her backyard. I couldn't teleport in Topside, but I could teleport in and out of my domain to Topside. It was kind of a hassle to use my domain as a nexus, but whatever.

"You little fucker! This is no time for stupid magic tricks." She was running into the backyard with the frying pan.

"Promise first, and I'll take you to them." I disappeared in another cloud of red smoke, touched my domain, and went back into the kitchen. I opened the fridge door and took out more lemonade. What she did with lemonade was somehow better than any other lemonade I'd ever had. I drank some more.

"You little," she started, but she had to stop. "I'm exhausted. I don't want to be arrested for assaulting you."

"Wise," I commented.

She gave me a glare, but she said, "Okay, I promise to obey you if you take me to my children." She let the frying pan go.

"Done." I snapped my fingers and brought her to my domain. I had to admit that fucking her was one of my many fantasies from the time I started getting boners, but time was of the essence. "You'll be assigned a spot to patrol or defend by Amber, my First Guardian. Your daughters are here. If the castle falls, then..." I stopped giving her the quick version of what was going on. I actually didn't know what happened to my harem if my caput fell and I became a vassal. Did I keep it or did my new overlord take my chicks? I wished there was an information button!

"You don't want the castle to fall," I finished lamely.

"As long as you take me to my daughters, I'll pick up a stupid sword or whatever." She was looking at my fortress with an expression that said she'd just smelled a whiff of poo. I remembered that I hadn't told anybody to clean up after Rufus, and then I frowned. Rufus had actually not had anything to clean up. I thought that I'd deliberately reset Evelynn and someone else so that they didn't anything else, but maybe everyone was in a state of suspension in Hell. I tried to remember if I'd set up a kitchen with food in it, and I realized I hadn't. People could eat and drink here, but they didn't need to. It reminded me of the old tale of Hades and Persephone, where she was doomed to stay in Hell for half of the year because she had eaten six pomegranate seeds. I didn't think that eating in my domain came with those consequences, but there wasn't a ton of food hanging around to try it out. I remembered the filet mignon I'd made for myself. Was I going to be bound here for half a year?

It was awesome here, I had to admit. All I had to do was snap my fingers and whatever I wanted appeared. I could teleport around my own domain and teleport from my virtual life Topside to my domain instantly. But being trapped was a different matter. There wasn't an informative guidebook. I couldn't just walk into a bookstore and get tips on how to advance in the game. I had to think about all of that later, because I looked back at the MILF that I'd brought back. I snapped my fingers and dressed her in what I thought housewives should wear.

She looked down at herself and screeched, "What am I wearing?"

"What you should wear every day." I admired the French maid costume I'd put on her. The French maid must be really slutty, because the skirt revealed a lot of inches of luscious, pinchable ass. Her tits were barely covered, too, because the costume was low cut and her nipples were almost peeking out.

"I'm not going to wear this!" she shouted at me.

"You agreed to obey me," I countered.

She bit her lip. "But you promised to bring me to my daughters."

"Of course." I snapped my fingers and took us to the gate.

"What have you done to them?!" she screeched in my ear. Her daughters were still on the spanking benches.

"Master is here." Cecilia turned her head as much as she could. "Mama?"

"My poor babies!" she tried to unlatch the bonds, her hands scrabbling around, trying to figure out how to undo them. Since I'd put them on with my mind, the only way to get them off was for me to do undo them. "What a monster!"

Was I a monster? I'd tied down willing women. Yes, I'd used my pheromones on them, but they still had free will.

"We like being here, Mama," Cecilia said as softly as she could.

"Like it!" she sounded like she was going to faint in a second. "It's so degrading."

"It's freedom," Cheyenne told her adoptive mother. "And I don't have to worry about the sleazy team owner. Or going to practice and being paid less than minimum wage."

"That's true," Cecilia said. I'd read some news articles about sketchy team owners and some class-action lawsuits. Cheerleaders were beautiful but there was always some new shit in the news about things they had to put up with. I'd never connected those stories with Cecilia and Cheyenne. They were so beautiful that it seemed like nothing bad could happen to them, like extraordinary beauty was some kind of protection. I guessed not.

I looked at their mother, who was struggling to understand what was going on. I got the impression that they'd talked to her about sleazy men and work conditions before, which meant that she understood that being Guardians for me was actually a step up for her adopted daughters.

Eventually, she said, "If that's what you want." Her shoulders slumped. She always had great posture, so it was a shock to see her looking so defeated.

"Ma'am," I said, pretending to be the kind of gentleman I wasn't, considering that I'd dressed her in a French maid's costume, can I see you to your post now that you've met your daughters?"

She gave me a long, searching look before she finally said, "Yes." I snapped my fingers and got us back into the security room, where Amber seemed to be recalibrating all of our sensors or something.

"New meat," I told Amber. "Be kind to her. She's Cecilia and Cheyenne's mother."

"Those girls you put at the gate?" Amber asked. She looked the MILF up and down, licking her lips. "Well, hello."

"Is this some kind of sex club?" she asked, stiffening yet pushing her generous boobs up.

"No," I said. "Or if it is, it's one centered around me."

"Let me show you around," Amber said. "I've got this, boss."

As soon as I saw Amber take her arm and lead her out of the room, I sat back in a chair and reviewed everything Amber had done. It looked like we were in good shape. I needed to think of more women to bring to defend the caput. I also needed a strike team. For some reason, my mind went to Hailey.

I swallowed hard. It was never easy to think about Hailey. I used to dream stupid dreams about her. She was beautiful in a girl-next-door kind of way. She'd asked me to homecoming our freshman year of high school. She was so far out of my league that I almost said no, sure that it was some kind of joke. And of course later I found out that I'd been a dumb patsy. Things hadn't ended well between us, but for some reason I knew that if I had a strike team to take other player's caputs, I'd want her to be the captain of it. I snapped my fingers.

HAILEY THE PET PORTRAITIST

S uddenly I was back in the used Taurus that I'd used in high school. I'd bought it myself with the money I'd saved working for a tech repair company over the summer before my senior year. It got the job done. It was reliable and got me to school, even if it was this weird mustard yellow color that didn't do my dating life any favors.

Back then, I'd been Facebook official with Hailey, who was my definition of a perfect ten. She had long blonde hair with a hint of red in it, large green eyes, and naturally red lips. She was the perfect height for me, too, even if she dodged me every time that I tried to kiss her. I didn't understand why she'd asked me out in the first place until graduation. My blood boiled when I remembered how humiliated I'd been.

———

"SWEETIE," my mom called, "can you go find Hailey? I want some pictures of the two of you."

"Sure, Mom," I told her. I went to hunt for Hailey. It wasn't easy to find people in the crowd of a crazy number of people who were out here taking pictures in their graduation caps and gowns. She wasn't that short, but there were too many people for me to just shout her name. I saw the distinctive dreadlocks of Hailey's best friend, Camille, and headed towards her. Even if she didn't know where Hailey was, I imagined that Hailey would figure out a way to get to her. We weren't allowed to have cell phones at graduation, which was dumb because we needed to find our families afterwards.

"Ugh, I know, he's the worst," I heard as I approached. I didn't know who they were talking about, but some instinct made me hang back a little. One of my classmates had a dad who was a former professional football player, so there was plenty of cover. I was anonymous in a sea of people dressed exactly like me.

"Why the hell are you dating a loser like Felix anyway?" Camille asked as she took a selfie of the two of them. "Like, maybe he'll grow up to work in a middle class boring white collar job where he can be an Excel monkey. That's okay for some people but..."

"He's nice," my girlfriend Hailey said. "You can't post that one! My hair is a disaster."

"Shut up. You have stick straight hair. I would kill to have your hair."

"It can never hold a curl," Hailey replied, pouting for the camera. "Anyway, I have to date him because my mom is so strict. She said that if I ever felt interested in a boy, I had to bring him home to meet her first."

"So you picked Felix?"

"Well, yeah," Hailey confirmed, making my stomach sink. "Can you imagine anyone more boring?"

"No," Camille snorted. "I don't think it's possible."

I felt like I was going to barf. All the dates that I took her on, all the dances that I'd been with her to, all the boring Bible study sessions that were literally Bible study sessions that I'd attended for her, all of it was a stupid waste. I'd used my money to pay for my car, sure, but a lot of the money also went into dating her, because I always paid. She never even liked me at all. I was just a stupid doll to her, someone to make her mom feel safe. I'd heard enough and went back to my mom. I told her that I was sick, and we'd gone home. I'd broken up with Hailey through a phone call the next day. She didn't really care and hung up on me while I was explaining why.

I HADN'T SEEN Hailey since graduation day. But I could see myself driving to her house and being on her street. How did the game know so much about me?

"Bye, Mom," I could hear her saying. I saw her mom's next-year Lexus SUV driving off. I parked my old used Taurus where it always went, on the curb.

"Felix?" Hailey asked, confused. I was confused, too, frankly. I'd upgraded once I got a real job. Why did I have a Taurus? It was so old school that Ford soon wouldn't even be making them anymore.

I got out of my car. "Hi."

"Uh, excuse me, but... What the hell are you doing here?" Hailey hadn't changed much. Her tits got bigger, I guess, and her hair was a little shorter. But overall, she was the same teenage heartbreaker who never let me kiss her.

"Why are you at home in the middle of the day?" I countered. I looked at my watch. "It's just past noon."

"I'm a painter," she replied. "I take photographs of subjects and paint from home."

"I didn't know that you went to art school. I thought that you were going to major in political science." Hailey loved diving into politics and stuff.

"I did. I have a poli sci degree. So I could go to law school, work for a political campaign, or do something else. Now I'm a professional painter."

"That's cool, I guess." I didn't understand why I was here. Hailey didn't have anything to fix. Sure, she was still living at home, but half of my high school class still lived with their parents. It was easier to stay with your parents than find your own place, and most of them did chores and stuff to share the load equally. I wasn't saying that I'd be happy in that situation, just that I knew people who were.

"So why are you here?"

"I was in the neighborhood," I replied.

"You still have your car from high school?" Hailey asked me, wrinkling her nose. "You should get a paint job for it at least."

"I sold it," I told her. "I'm not sure why it's here."

"Uh, are you okay?" she asked me. "Do I need to call someone?" She looked at me as if I'd escaped from the loony bin or something.

"No," I told her. "I'm just having a weird couple of days." I didn't know how to explain what was going on to her. I probably didn't even want to. High school was so long ago, but sometimes I wondered about her. Did she find a better, less boring version of me to bring home to her mother? Had she gotten married? Did she have 2.5 kids and a dog?

It looked like she hadn't gotten married. No dog. No kids.

"You look different," Hailey said. "Have you been working out?"

I couldn't tell her the truth. I couldn't tell her that I'd chosen my avatar and had gotten in way over my head inside of a game. Maybe this whole thing was some kind of weird dream. I hadn't talked to Hailey for so long that I kind of thought she'd forget that I even existed. She hadn't reached out.

"Sure," I responded. Both of us kind of looked at our feet.

"So..." Hailey said.

"I should go," I replied, feeling as awkward as the 18-year-old boy who never got a goodnight kiss from his ultra-religious girlfriend. She was smoking hot but it was all for looking, never touching.

"Okay, bye." Hailey sounded relieved. I started walking away when I saw something out of the corner of my eye. "Is that a painting of a dog?"

Hailey wasn't a true redhead. However, she had fair skin and a tendency to turn bright red when she was upset or embarrassed. I watched her face turn the color of a vine-ripened tomato. "Yes."

"When you said you were a professional painter..."

"I'm a pet portraitist."

"A what?" I yanked on my ear. I couldn't have heard her correctly.

"Rich people are crazy about their pets," she explained. "I did one while I was still in school just as a side thing and the lady had me do her other two dogs. Word got around..."

"So instead of being an aide for a senator or something, you paint dogs?"

"I'm my own boss. I sign all of my paintings. My clients are generally happy enough to talk about my work and I'm booked for the next three years with a waiting list."

"Damn." I guessed I could see a little more clearly now why I'd been planted here. She still lived at home with her mom. She painted pictures of dogs for a living. She could be happy, I guessed, but I could kind of sense that she wasn't.

"Do you think I could have a glass of water? It's kind of a hot day."

"Yeah, sure, come on in."

I walked through the door that I'd walked through countless times as a teenager. Everything was exactly as I'd last seen it. The paint had faded a little bit, but it still smelled like sunshine and the daises that Hailey's mom always kept in the kitchen. Hailey filled up a glass of water from their fridge and handed it to me. I took a sip and set it down.

"Hailey, I have a question."

"Go for it." She was hugging herself now. I realized that she wasn't wearing a bra. I could see the points of her nipples. Maybe she was cold from being outside and moving indoors where there was air conditioning.

"Did you imagine a life like this for yourself when you got a college degree? I mean, I knew that you painted, but..."

She laughed. It was a tiny bit bitter. "Did I think that I'd be painting fat dogs for rich people who wanted to pay me more than my mom's monthly salary for each portrait? No."

"If you could do anything, what would it be?"

"I'd travel the world and paint landscapes. I always did landscapes growing up, but there's not really a market for those. Everyone does landscapes."

"You've tapped into a good market."

Hailey ran a hand through her hair. I noticed that she had a smudge of paint on her thumb that was transferred to her hair, leaving a brown streak. "Yeah, I guess."

I should've been used to it by now, but I still hesitated. Some long-forgotten part of me was desperate for Hailey's approval and attention. "I could help you with that."

"What, you know someone who wants to buy a shitload of landscapes?" she asked, but her voice had a hard, sarcastic edge.

"I could help you travel and paint landscapes if you really wanted," I told her.

"Yeah, right," Hailey bit off. "I think you should go."

"I'm being serious," I told her. I took off my shirt.

"What the fuck are you doing?" Hailey

screeched. But then she stopped in her tracks. "That's new."

"What, my six pack?" I grinned at her.

"Your everything," Hailey replied, gesturing at my body. "You're all..."

"I can offer your heart's desire. Just hear me out."

Hailey looked at the glowing green clock on the stove. "You have ten minutes."

I wouldn't need ten minutes. "Okay, so here's the story. I got fired from my job and had a bunch of spare time. I ran into Gareth, you remember him?"

"Yeah." She tilted her head a little bit, unsure why I was mentioning one of my old friends from high school neither of us had spoken to since then.

"So Gareth brought me to this place, and long story short, I have powers."

Hailey kind of gave me side-eye. "Powers?" Her tone was skeptical.

"Watch." I waved my hand at her fridge and opened it.

"That fridge has always been broken, and you know it."

I turned off the lights.

"Momentary power outage."

I grabbed her boob from 5 yards away. I didn't know why getting these powers meant that I felt comfortable crossing a line that I hadn't in high school.

"Hey!" But the last thing made her realize that I could manipulate objects without physically being in contact with them. "You can't grope me."

"I never touched you," I said, smiling. She got it now.

"So when I tell you that I want to travel and paint landscapes all around the world..."

"I can make it happen. Do you have any debts?"

Hailey shook her head. Of course she didn't. Her parents were loaded.

"Any pets? Any obligations?"

"I'm almost done with the current portrait. I just have to put on a layer of varnish and it'll be ready."

"Go do that."

"Now?" She looked at me, frowning.

"Right now."

"Okay..." Hailey went off to the room and starting doing things. I didn't know much about painting, so I just sat and watched her. Her ass looked perfect in the shorts she was wearing. They were made of some kind of cotton that looked soft and comfortable. Her shorts gripped her ass lovingly. I barely held myself back from pinching it while she finished the last thing she needed to do before she swore to serve me.

After a while, Hailey turned around and announced, "I'm done!"

"Call them. Tell them to pick it up from the house."

She did exactly what I commanded, which was probably a good sign. I waited while she gave them instructions on how to send money to her.

"Are you done with everything you need to do now?" I checked.

"Yeah. Uh, will I see my parents again?"

I wasn't willing to wait for her to pen a heartfelt note to her parents explaining her absence and her sojourn into my corner of Hell. "Yes." After her contract was done, she would be free to do as she wished.

"Okay. I need to pack or something..."

"No." I corrected her. "You don't need to pack." She didn't understand the extent of my powers yet.

"Then I'm ready," she said, rubbing her palms on her shorts and stepping closer to me.

"I can you offer you what you've dreamed of. What will you do in order to achieve your dreams?"

"Anything," she said.

"Swear it. Tell me that you'll do anything to achieve my dreams." I extended my hand to her to seal our handshake deal.

"I swear to you that I'll do anything to achieve my dreams." She put her small hand in mine. "Make my dreams come true." I could see the fear in her eyes, but she'd sworn herself to me.

I lifted my hand and teleported us to my domain and then to Lake Tekapo, New Zealand. I'd seen pictures of it and heard it mentioned on some documentaries about New Zealand.

"Holy shit," she said, letting go of my hand and kneeling on the ground. She plucked a flower from the ground. "Is this real?"

"It's real." I liked watching her kneel in front of me.

"What do I have to do in return? There's no such thing as a free lunch." She understood that she'd made a deal with me.

"You're one of my Guardians now."

"Guardians?" She pulled her brows together.

"You have to defend my fortress from other people for the next three years and serve me during that time. After that, I'll transport you to wherever you want to see. You won't have to worry about airfare, accommodation, food, or paint supplies. I'll provide everything." I could give her anything that she wanted with the new powers I'd attained.

"I'm in." She got to her feet. "I don't know

why I believe you, but I do." Her hand rested on my arm.

"Because you know that I'll keep my promise to you." I lifted my hand again to take her back to my fortress, but then I remembered what I wanted to do, something that I'd never been allowed to.

"I'm going to kiss you." Before she realized what I was going to do, I planted one on her soft lips. I felt her gasp, but I lifted my hand and teleported us back to the fortress before she could react.

She took a few steps back from me and opened her mouth. But whatever she was going to say died before she got a single word out. "Wow. This fortress is yours?"

"Yeah, and it's your home for the next three years."

She spun in a slow circle. I'd brought us to the main courtyard. I could see that Amber had worked hard on building the main building while I was gone. She apparently wanted to use a lot of gold. I hadn't really paid attention to all the stuff that she'd had me snap into existence.

"It's like walking into El Dorado." Hailey was still looking at the roof.

"Yeah, that was my intention." Or Amber's, anyway. I didn't give a fuck about decorations.

"I gotta say, this place is way better than where you used to live."

I shrugged. "I guess." The house in the real world was real. This house was something built by my imagination and the imagination of... imaginary versions of real people? I didn't understand why

NPCs were able to create, but this game was really well-built.

"So... where do I stay? What do I do?" She twisted her long hair into a bun and secured it, like she always did when she was nervous. It was as if she needed to do something with her hands.

"You have to talk to Amber about your duties. She'll find something for you." I thought about changing Hailey's clothes, but I liked the paint-splattered shirt and shorts. I surreptitiously shortened the hems by about two inches so I could see her bare midriff and a little more thigh. I didn't shrink them so much that she would notice quickly, though.

Hailey swallowed hard. "There's another girl?"

"There are a lot of other girls," I explained to her. "You're one of the Guardians."

"You keep saying that, but I don't know what it means."

"It means that you're one of us," I heard Amber say. She had creeped up from behind us.

Hailey jumped a foot in the air. "Ahh!"

Amber snickered, covering her mouth with one hand. "Hey, newbie."

Hailey looked Amber up and down. "Who is she?"

"Amber," I said. "Hailey will need to be given the tour and some kind of duty. She's a painter."

"Another useless bitch," Amber grumbled. "At some point, you need to get some chicks with real skills instead of women you want to stick your dick inside."

"Shut it," I told Amber. Her mouth immediately closed. She was obviously trying to open her jaw, but she couldn't. It was good to have powers here.

"Uh, what's happening to her?" Hailey was staring at Amber while Amber clawed at her jaw.

"While you're in the fortress, I'm the master of the domain. I'm the laird here. You have to obey my commands."

She watched Amber still trying to claw her jaw open. "So if I disobey..."

"Don't." I smiled at her. "You told me that you were in. We made a deal. Three years of serving me and defending my holdings before I send you on the trip of your dreams with whatever you want."

"How long will the trip of my dreams last, though? I mean, you said that I wouldn't have to worry about anything."

"And you won't. I'll let you travel and paint for as long as you want. When you tell me that you're done, then you'll be done."

"What if I want to paint landscapes until I'm 100?"

"Then that's within the bounds of our agreement."

"That seems too good to be true for 3 years of servitude."

"Here's the thing. Over time, I'm going to upgrade. You're a good starter Guardian."

Hailey frowned at me. "What?"

"You're just a starter version," I said, running a hand through my hair. "But later, I'll get some war-ladies or something to match my new warlord status. As I level up, my holdings have to be defended by better people. Right now, it's about body count."

"You don't want me?"

"I only need you for what you can offer."

"I don't know what to say." Hailey looked a little offended by the idea that I didn't want her specifically. She thought that she was special. To be fair, she was. I had acquired her for an actual purpose. But I also wasn't above getting a little bit back at her after the way that she'd treated me in high school. I would train her for our domain and kick her to the curb when I'd outgrown her. She looked really offended now and I didn't even have to really care. The tables had turned. Now she was at my mercy.

But as fun as this was, I needed to get more guardians. I tried to think of the people I'd want to add to my harem. Immediately, the image of Daphne bent over my desk, with her tits in my face, popped into my mind. She was such a fucking cocktease and it had taken her far. I wanted to add her to my harem. Maybe it was easier for her to seduce our boss with her fantastic body, but there was some element of planning in landing such a big prize. She would be a great addition to my harem and I knew that she could think strategically.

DAPHNE

I snapped my fingers and reappeared in my old cubicle. They'd taken away my computer. All that was left were a bunch of binders from training sessions, a pair of scissors, and a couple pens. There was a half-used stack of Post-Its in one corner.

"Stop it, you animal!" I heard Daphne giggling. "We're at work."

"It's after work. When the cat's away, the mice will play."

I knew that voice. My mouth went dry as Xavier came into view.

"Where did Dan go?"

"He's having some kind of dinner with one of his former professors, that one who recommended Felix." Daphne didn't sound like she cared a lot about what her husband did after work.

"Glad that asshole is gone," I heard Xavier say. I didn't want to be a whiny little bitch and cry about my feelings, but it definitely shocked me just a little that the same guy who used to go to the sports bar around the corner from the office for happy hour with me was so glad that I was gone and called me an asshole.

"You want to fuck on the asshole's desk?" Their voices were getting closer.

I looked around for cover. Where could I possibly hide? There wasn't anywhere to hide, not in my cubicle. Then I remembered that I had powers and snapped my fingers to make myself invisible. I did it just in time, too, because a half second later Xavier was carrying Daphne into my cubicle.

"Your skirts drive me wild," he moaned, kissing her neck and setting her luscious ass on my desk. I hated both of them right now, but I also noticed how fucking hot Daphne looked, tousled, the buttons of her shirt undone, and her zipper sliding down. I swallowed really hard as Xavier tugged off her skirt and left it in a crumpled pile on the floor. I knew someone like Daphne would only wear the best, plus she owned half of a big business. She could afford anything she wanted, and what she wanted was barely there lace lingerie. I watched as Xavier tore off her panties with his teeth.

"You're such an animal," Daphne gasped. "Do you have any idea how much these cost?"

"Like you care," Xavier sneered. "Look at how soaking wet these are. You can afford to buy new ones every day for the rest of your life." He was holding up her shredded underwear. I could see the damp spot on them. And we all knew that it was true. After marrying the CEO, Daphne was set for life.

"Well, I might as well buy a new set since you just ruined half of it," Daphne said. She was smiling at Xavier. With her lipstick smeared and her hair tousled, she looked like someone who was down for a good roll in the hay.

Xavier apparently understood what she meant, because he was quickly undoing the remaining buttons of her shirt before taking it off of her and tossing it into the corner where the Post-Its were. He grabbed a pair of scissors and sliced through the center part in the front, neatly severing a cute pink bow.

I didn't know if her tits were real. They were slightly wider than her body. Daphne was shaped like Jessica Rabbit, only with blonde hair. She had giant tits, a tiny waist, and hips that drew attention to every step that she took. Xavier leaned down to take a mouthful of Daphne's right tit and must have been biting her, because she kind of screamed in pleasure and pain.

"Fuck!" she panted. "Don't leave marks. I don't want my husband to know."

"That you are cheating on him with one of your employees?" Xavier asked. I watched as he forced her thighs apart and then slid two fingers inside of her cunt, making her body arch. "That you love to come on my fingers while I stroke your clit?" I watched as his thumb circled her clit. "That you like it rougher and dirtier than he'll ever be able to manage?" Daphne was gasping for air as Xavier thrust his fingers even deeper. I saw as she writhed in place, Xavier putting one hand on her throat. "You love every second of this, Daphne."

I could see from the shame and arousal on her face that she did love it. And I wondered how long it had been going on. Xavier and I hadn't been on a happy hour run for maybe a few months. Clearly today wasn't the first time that they'd fucked. She was orgasming on my desk, helpless before Xavier. His pupils were so dilated he looked like he wouldn't be able to pass a drug test. He was getting off on this power play, this reversal of positions where he had our boss's wife helpless on my desk.

"I'm going to turn you over," he said into her ear, although I could hear him perfectly. "I'm going to fuck you over this desk with your hands tied and your mouth gagged. Won't you like that?"

"Yes," she moaned.

Xavier pulled out a zip tie from his pocket and secured her wrists. Then he positioned her the way that he wanted her.

"What do you want?" he asked her.

"I want your cock," she muttered.

"I can't hear you," he replied.

"I want your cock," she shouted. "Give it to me!"

She sounded like a spoiled little brat. I watched as he spanked one of her ass cheeks. "What's the magic word?" he demanded.

"Please!" she begged. "Please give it to me."

She screamed as he fucked into her in one brutal stroke, hands on her hips to pin her in place. There was no easing in. There was no real concern for her comfort. I knew that she was soaking wet from the scent in the air and her the wet spot on her torn underwear, but wow. Xavier was slamming into her. I thought that he was fucking her with enough force to knock the cubicle walls over.

"You're such a fucking slut," he told her as he kept hammering her cunt. "You love it when your husband is away and you can show your true colors. You don't want to wear cardigans and skirts. Bodies like yours should never be covered up. The only thing you should wear is my cum."

The sounds of them fucking took over. Xavier was beyond speech before he shouted his own release, spilling into someone else's wife. When he pulled out, I could see his seed falling on the ground. He hadn't thrown her skirt away like he had thrown her shirt, so cum was dripping onto her skirt. He picked it up and cleaned her with it.

"Fuck you," she said, "why couldn't you find a paper towel?"

"Why not use your skirt when it's already stained with cum?"

She didn't have an answer for that. I could see the bite marks on her tits and places where he had left hand marks that would become bruises. "It's a miracle that Dan hasn't noticed," she said ruefully, looking at her tits.

"He only gives you some vanilla missionary, under the sheets, in the dark once a month," Xavier snorted. "And that's only if he doesn't have any business trips."

I saw her lips trembling. "You don't have to rub it in," she muttered. "Who knew that he was a limp dick?"

I didn't know if she was saying that Dan couldn't get it up or if the shininess had worn off of his new wife. I wondered if he understood her true colors now and regretted marrying the little gold digger. She had tears gathering in her eyes.

"Hey, I'm sorry," Xavier apologized, wrapping her in his arms and kissing her.

"Why should you be sorry?" she asked, her voice quivering. "It's the truth."

I understood then why a woman who had every material comfort would jeopardize it by fucking her employee. Sure, she could sue the shit out of Dan and walk away with 50% of everything, but the legal battle would be ugly. She was treading water, staying in place in a marriage with a man who didn't love her or plow her regularly. This stolen time, fucking Xavier in my cubicle while they badmouthed me, was her way of reclaiming some control. She'd set up her life so that she had millions of dollars at her disposal. She still wasn't happy.

I'd grown up with the idea that if you made enough money, you'd be okay and everything would fall into place. But looked at Daphne, I understood that having a hot trophy wife wasn't all it was

cracked up to be. Daphne was for looking, not necessarily touching. Their marriage was a damned waste of a sexy piece
of ass. I still thought that Xavier was a
dick, but I understood now why he'd risk
his job for a couple minutes of ecstasy.
He was giving her more than just semen.
Maybe he felt good being a white knight
who got to rescue the beautiful princess
from the tower guarded by a fire-
breathing dragon.

The looks that they were giving each
other were too intimate for me to be in-
truding on. I hadn't minded watching
them fuck, which kind of was like a live
sex show or watching porn. But
watching Daphne rest her head on his
shoulder showed me that Xavier was
giving her something she wasn't getting
at home. Yeah, dick, obviously, but also
some kind of tenderness. Xavier was her

gay best friend who also fucked her brains out while her hands were tied up and she was facedown. Both of them were getting something out of fucking.

Xavier obviously understood the need to change the topic. "I'm glad you fired Felix."

I stiffened when Daphne stretched, smiled at him, and said, "I know." She winked at that motherfucker.

Those assholes. I could almost feel the steam coming out of my ears. "I know that he would've gone to Dan about us as soon as he had more than just suspicions." Daphne was kissing Xavier's shoulder now, slowly rubbing his hands up and down his back and then going down to his ass to squeeze it.

The joke was on them, because I had no fucking clue that they'd been fucking each other before now. I'd lost my job because I seemed to know something that I had no idea about at all. Fucking perfect. They'd fired me for nothing at all. I knew that Daphne had been acting to protect herself, but I was pissed that they were able to kill my livelihood by fucking on company ground. If I knew what I knew now, I would go straight to Dan and convince him to divorce her ass. She was such a massive pain to deal with that I would've gotten rid of her if I'd had the chance. I hated to admit it, but she'd won by making her move first.

Even though it fucking sucked to be unemployed, Daphne understood the rules of war. I needed her to be one of my Guardians. I watched as Xavier fucked her with his fingers until she shuddered and came. She would've fallen down if Xavier hadn't had his hand in her cunt and his other hand on her ass. It was romantic in a dirty way.

Fun as watching live porn was, I didn't have a lot of time to waste. All the other women had consented to come to Hell with me. While Xavier was here, I didn't know how I was going to convince Daphne. I had to get rid of him first. How?

Inspiration struck and I snapped my fingers to get myself back to Hell. And then, for the first time since I'd been given these powers, I went somewhere in my memories of the real world that didn't include a hot chick.

MORE DAPHNE

When I'd gone back to Hell and gone from there to Dan, I looked around. I was in a fancy penthouse and there were two women in bed with Dan. Okay, now I knew why Daphne wasn't getting any. One of them was sucking his dick with enthusiasm and her hands tied behind her back with rope; the other one was humping his face and basically suffocating him while he ate her. I had no idea that my boss spent his free time fucking multiple women. Lucky bastard.

And then I walked around near the headboard. I could understand now why he was letting the girl sit on his face. The view of her tits moving was phenomenal. She had bigger tits than Kate Upton and could move her hips better than Shakira. I wiped my chin to make sure I didn't have embarrassing drool or anything. The girl on top of Dan had thrown her head back as she screamed her way through a climax while the girl who was tied up and sucking Dan's dick was now positioning herself to get the facial of a lifetime. He was painting her face and tits. The smile on her face said that she was enjoying every bit of it.

As fun as this was, it was clear to me that traveling to Dan and telling him that his wife was unfaithful was not going to have the impact that I'd hoped it would. I just was going to have to figure out a different way to convince Xavier to go away and Daphne to become one of my strategists.

I almost turned to go when I realized that Dan's phone was buzzing in the corner, unnoticed by the sweaty people on the bed. I walked over and took it before snapping myself to Hell and snapping myself into my next door neighbors' house. The mom and the girls were in Hell anyway. I read the text, which was some generic reminder from his secretary about an early meeting that he had to do tomorrow. The meeting was with a bunch of Dutch financiers and I kind of was puzzled why he would get money from Dutch venture capitalists when there was plenty of money available in the US.

But I shrugged it aside, not understanding how my boss was getting his money and not really caring. I guessed that if the meeting was with Russian financiers I'd care, but otherwise it had no impact on my life beyond getting my final paycheck. In the end, it might turn out that Daphne giving me the boot had worked out for the best. I had no idea how dysfunctional my company was until I was outside of it.

I tapped out a message on Dan's phone to go to Daphne, whose name had a little unicorn emoji next to it. It was obvious that she'd keyed it in herself. I went for something short and sweet: Come home.

It sounded like he mostly ignored her outside of work, and maybe inside of work, so just those two words might freak her out. I was looking through their texting history and the last time that they'd texted about anything was three months ago. Considering that they'd only been married for a few months, it wasn't a great sign for their marriage. I snapped myself back to Hell and then back to my cubicle.

———

DAPHNE WAS HAVING a full-blown panic attack. She was gasping for air on the floor while Xavier was kneeling next to her. I could see the glowing screen of the phone in her hand.

"He knows," she wheezed. "He knows!"

"It's okay, babe," Xavier comforted her. "There's no way. He just probably sprained his ankle or something while golfing."

I didn't know why she was fucking someone else if it was going to freak her out this much, but I didn't understand women anyway. Xavier helped her sit up and Daphne seemed to be able to breathe after a few minutes.

"I have to go home," she moaned. "I have to face the music."

"Good luck," Xavier told her, pulling her to her feet and kissing her, his hands clamping on her ass and pulling her against him. "You'll be fine." He zipped her up in a dress that she'd had in her giant purse sitting in the hallway, since her clothing was already destroyed and/or stained.

After a few more kisses, Daphne was walking away, her purse in her hand and a determined look on her face. I'd set some wheels in motion but Xavier and I both watched as she sauntered away. Only a few minutes ago she'd been in a crumpled heap on the ground. Now she looked like the boss I'd hated ever since she'd married Dan.

Xavier was shaking his head as he went to the bathroom to clean up. I wanted to say something to him about what a two-faced asshole he was, but I had bigger fish to fry.

———

I snapped myself to Hell and then to their house. I'd been there a few times pre-Daphne when Dan had a couple poker nights. We'd order a giant platter of wings from a sports bar nearby. Dan would supply a shitload of beer. We were prohibited from playing for money so we played for different colors of candy instead of having legit chips, but it was still fun and a good way to let loose on a Friday night. Those poker nights had stopped the minute that Dan had put a ring on Daphne's finger. She said that it was sexist to have poker nights with only men and proposed having a bowling team or something. Daphne was a buzzkill.

Daphne was in the kitchen, pulling out some margarita mix and tequila. It looked like she had to be liquored up in order to talk to her own husband. Jesus Christ. How had I missed this? Dan wasn't coming home, obviously, since his phone was in my hand while I watched Daphne turn on the blender. She poured herself a generous amount of tequila like a 21-year-old college student who was on Spring Break in Cabo. I saw it disappear. That lady could suck like a vacuum cleaner. I could feel my body responding to the idea of making Daphne use that enthusiasm elsewhere.

When her giant cup was empty, I saw her go to the couch. She had started crying again, which was a boner killer. Something was seriously wrong with her, more than just the infidelity on both sides of the marriage. I could see that she was in a terrible mood. Yes, she was alone now and I could approach her. However, if I did, then she'd probably tell me no and I'd have wasted my time and magic on someone who didn't want to come back with me. Sometimes this game was way too hard. At first, I thought that it was about acquiring chicks for an army, which I was totally fine with. Now the game had progressed to a level that was beyond my ability. I hadn't even been able to convince Daphne that I could keep my job. Now I was supposed to convince her to come to Hell. Ridiculous.

What the hell was I supposed to do? Immediately after wondering, I saw a new quest pop up. Weird. It was like they were reading my mind or something.

Own the Golddigger
Daphne is a lonely golddigger married to a cheating husband. Convince her to join your army and receive 1000 XP.

It sounded like a lot of XP, but I wasn't sure what XP was for in this game. It had been a while since I leveled up. Maybe the lack of new quests and lack of XP were part of it. I couldn't even remember what level. I wanted to own Daphne anyway. I went to the couch where she was curled up. She was blowing her nose into a tissue when I appeared.

"What the fuck!" she screamed when she saw me appear out of thin air. "Get out of here before I call the police, you stalker!" she shouted at me. I ducked as she threw her giant cup at me. I saw ice falling out of the cup as it hit the wall behind me.

Should I turn invisible again? I was nervous in a way that I hadn't been when I had picked up Amber and Bianca, my first two. Wait, I had an ideal. "Back in a minute."

She opened her mouth to say something but I was already gone. One snap to Hell where I could wrap my arm around Bianca's waist, one snap back to Daphne.

"Look," I told Daphne. Bianca had burrowed into my shoulder and was now kissing my neck. It was turning me on but the look on Daphne's face was half fear and half arousal. Bianca was now nibbling my neck in a very distracting way.

"What have you done to her? Is that a sex robot?"

"I'm not a robot," Bianca retorted, turning so that she could talk to Daphne and also rub her fine ass on my dick. "I'm his."

"His what?" Daphne asked.

"His," Bianca said, humming a little and closing her eyes. She was clearly having a good time dry humping me. In another minute, I could fuck her. I just needed Daphne to get on board first.

"I don't know what freaky shit you've gotten into, Felix, but I want no part in it. Now go before my husband gets home."

I could see her nipples trying to poke through her shirt. "You're aroused." Or cold, but from the guilt and flush showing on her face, she was turned on.

"Get out," she hissed, getting to her feet. "And take your whore with you."

"Bianca," I purred, lifting her out of my lap even though she struggled, "why don't you make the lady feel good?"

Bianca's face became hungry as she prowled towards Daphne. She kind of body tackled her back onto the couch, straddling her. The view was great.

Bianca's ass was perfect and her thick thighs were bracketing Daphne's long legs. I wished that I could take a picture and make it last. She was grinding her horny cunt on Daphne's leg while literally ripping Daphne's shirt so that she could start biting her breasts. Bianca was like an unleashed animal going wild. Daphne's clothing was torn to shreds as Bianca acted like covered skin was a major sin. Soon, Daphne wasn't wearing anything worth mentioning. Bianca's face was buried between Daphne's thighs as she maneuvered Daphne into a 69 position. Daphne's face showed that she was on the verge of orgasming.

I had to make my move. "Bianca, stop."

Without hesitation or whining, Bianca pulled away from Daphne.

"What? Why?" Daphne howled. Her hand was going towards her clit to finish herself off. I moved forward to pull it away.

"You're not going to be able to get yourself to finish."

"I'm used to it. I always have to do it when I fuck Dan. He thinks that two pumps are as long as sex needs to last."

TMI. I didn't want to know what my former boss was like in bed. "You can't finish yourself off."

I could see her writhing helplessly as Bianca and I looked at her. I wondered if Daphne had a little bit of voyeurism in her. Her body was wet and her nipples were hard still. "Please," she moaned. "I'll do anything."

"Anything?"

"Yes," she replied, still trying to pull her hands from mine.

"Swear to me. Swear to obey me." I wouldn't have asked that of her even a half hour ago. But things had changed once I brought Bianca into the mix. Women understood a female body's pleasure points. Bianca could go down on Daphne and laser target her hot spots. Watching women go to town on each other was quite an informative experience.

"I promise. I swear," Daphne panted. "Please let me finish."

After she'd given me her consent, I made a movement with my hand for Bianca to finish Daphne off while I held Daphne's hands in place. Bianca used a hard and fast rhythm with her tongue to push Daphne over the cliff. Daphne screamed

as she orgasmed, her entire body con-
vulsing. Bianca was thrown clear of
Daphne as if she'd been riding a bucking
bronco. She didn't seem hurt as she got
to her feet, but what game would include
real injuries? The laws of physics didn't
seem to apply in this game. If anything,
Bianca's lack of injuries served to highlight that we were inside of my memories, not in the real world, although I
wondered why Daphne had mixed herself a fish bowl of margaritas. I had never
seen her drink that much booze. While I
had been inside of the house, I hadn't
really been here when Daphne was
drinking like a sorority girl turning 21.

Moving back to the couch, Bianca kept
going because I hadn't told her to stop. I
watched as Daphne squirmed and cried
out beneath her. If we were in the real
world, Daphne would to leave one hell

of a wet spot on the couch. But we were inside of a virtual projection of my memories, which meant that there was no mess to clean up.

"Stop," Daphne moaned weakly. "It's too much."

"You've sworn to obey me and you'll like it." I kept watching as Bianca continued to coax Daphne's body into orgasms she didn't want but had already consented to. Daphne's face was a mixture of elation and exhaustion. I wasn't going to turn Daphne into something like Evelynn, since one Evelynn was enough. I needed Daphne as part of my army. I needed her loyalty to be directly to me, not coerced by having Bianca edge her.

"Stop," I told Bianca. Unlike when Daphne gave the order, Bianca obeyed me. She wiped her lips with the back of her hand and then licked the cream like a little cat. For some reason, the motion reminded me of Faelyn. But I didn't have time to dive into that right now.

"We're going to leave your house," I told Daphne a half second before I snapped my fingers.

"Where are we?" she yelled as we appeared in Hell. She was wearing the shreds of her clothing and not much else. She tried to cover up her giant tits with one hand, which only made her cleavage deeper.

"My place," I told her. "Welcome to mi casa."

Daphne was trying to walk, look, and cover her tits at the same time. She was only partially successful. "I want clothes," she said, her voice strained. "I'm not going to walk around with my tits out."

Being dedicated to the comfort of my harem, I snapped my fingers and handed her an outfit.

She stared at it and said, "Not that."

"Why not?" I asked. I'd always imagined her as a little bit of a dominatrix. She'd been able to talk Dan into marrying her, despite his better judgment, and she wanted her tits covered. Wish granted.

"It doesn't cover anything!" she snarled at me.

"You wanted your tits to be covered. The outfit covers your tits."

"There are like two inches of leather to cover my breasts," she argued. "That's not covering my tits, that's pretending to cover my tits."

"Listen, sweetheart," I said, putting an arm around Bianca who practically orgasmed at the contact, purring very quietly. "You're in my domain now and you've sworn to obey me."

I snapped my fingers again and she was wearing the black leather outfit. It was made of straps and kind of looked like a sexy spiderweb on her. I could see the top, sides, and bottoms of her tits with only part of her areolae covered.

"Get it off," Daphne screamed, twisting and trying to figure out how to take the spiderweb outfit off.

"Good luck," I told her, smiling down at Bianca while her hand reached for my dick. I'd made sure that it was nearly impossible for her to get off by herself. She'd need my help and be trapped in it forever. She was wearing a crotchless bikini bottom made of leather. I snapped my fingers, leaving Daphne in the court-yard. I'd send Amber out in a bit to intro-duce Daphne to the rest of the harem. Daphne was a good strategist. However, I had to teach her where she fit in the hierarchy to begin with. She could never forget that she served me and that her desires were subordinate to my own. She wasn't a natural submissive, not like Bianca, which made the whole experi-ence just a little bit richer. I thought about Dan coming home to an empty house and knowing that Daphne wasn't coming back, even though her car was there. Maybe the delight that I felt, the schadenfreude, was evil, but this was a virtual reality game. In real life, Daphne was probably waiting for him naked at home, ready to suck his cock and make him feel like a king. It was depressing to think about real life, though, so I stroked

Bianca's soft hair. I'd learned my lesson about modifying anybody too much. I didn't want to waste any modification points.

"Bianca," I said, running my fingers through her hair. She looked up to me, ready to please. It was all over her face. "Could you braid your hair into two handlebars for me?"

"Right away, Master," she replied. Even though I could've snapped my fingers to make it happen, I loved watching Bianca thrust out her tits to braid her own hair. While it might've been easier to ask one of the other girls in the harem to braid it, she didn't ask for help and I didn't summon anyone. It was strangely intimate to be here alone with her in one of the rooms in my fortress and watch her tits jiggle as she braided her long hair into two braids, one on each side. As soon as she was done, I snapped my fingers and put ribbons on the end of each one. I had two women who were school-girl fantasies, but Bianca was something different. I changed her outfit so that she was wearing a pink ballerina's tutu. Those things were stretchy and thin, and this one was basically transparent. It was too small for her giant tits, so she was spilling everywhere. She had on sparkling ballet shoes with those criss-crossing straps. I wondered then if her own desires played into what happened in the game, because I definitely hadn't thought of that element.

"I love my crystal-encrusted shoes, Master," Bianca said breathily. She slid to her knees in front of me, grabbed my dick, and started giving me the best head of my life. If I hadn't been next to a bed, it would've made me fall. Instead, I seated

myself on the bed, grabbed her handlebars, and went along for the ride. Bianca
knew my body well enough now that she
could play me like a violin. If she weren't
so devoted to me, it might've been a problem. Women had been getting what they
wanted since the dawn of time by pussy-
whipping men. The blow job I was getting right now would've made me one of
those suckers if Bianca had ever given it
to me in real life. But outside of this
game, she'd sold herself to some guy and
was a sugar baby. I didn't have the
money to maintain one of those. I took
my illicit pleasures where I could.

Before I shot, I pulled her head out of
my lap and spun her. She wasn't heavier
than a pillow, since the laws of physics
didn't really apply the same way in here
that they did in real life. I arranged her
in my lap so that her knees were on the

bed on the outside of my thighs. I reached to check how wet she was. She wasn't wearing any panties. I eased myself into her and she rocked on me in a steady rhythm that entranced me. I watched her braids move as she moved on top of me like a cyclone. I slid one hand around her to grab her tits, which made her clench tighter around my dick. I wondered then if I should just devote all my resources to defending my fortress, but I didn't. I knew it was only a matter of time before someone tried to steal my harem. Despite the temptation to fuck all their brains out nonstop, I'd end up becoming a vassal to someone else if I didn't attack preemptively.

With a sigh, I let myself go. Bianca cried out as I touched her clit and forced her to orgasm on top of me. She was a lot of fun. With a sigh, I snapped us into a shower, cleaned us up, and put Bianca to sleep. I had taken a lot out of her when I'd fucked her and asked her to convince Daphne with me. She deserved to rest.

I snapped myself into the control room in time to see Amber glaring at Daphne. Both of them were both alpha women used to being in charge.

"Thank you, Master," Amber said, the sweetness in her voice making me take a step back. I knew that tone of voice. It meant that she was about to give someone a beating. I'd learned enough to avoid annoying or frustrating her this much. One time, we'd gone to Five Guys and they'd forgotten to put the Cajun seasoning on her fries. She flipped her shit and screamed at the manager for a solid 10 minutes. "Why don't you tell this little bitch her place?"

"I'm in charge," Daphne countered, her face set. "Tell her, Felix."

"The fact that you don't know my name says it all," I told Daphne. Her jaw dropped as Amber smirked. "She's my First Guardian and in charge of keeping every other harem member in line."

"Harem?" Daphne asked.

"Surely you didn't think that you were Master's only slave." Amber was enjoying this too much. She stood up and slid her hands all over me, pinching my ass which made me give her a look. She only grinned in response.

"You saw Bianca," I told Daphne. "You swore yourself to me. What did you think?"

"I thought," Daphne replied through clenched teeth, "that I'd be special. And now I'm finding out you've enslaved any old whore."

Amber let go of me and dove for Daphne. Instead of breaking them up, which I should've done, I snapped my fingers so that we were in a mud pit. Daphne was still wearing her leather spiderweb and Amber soon was wearing a string bikini which barely covered anything at all, definitely not a lot when she was rolling around in the mud. Watching them go at each other was more fun than watching Amber and Bianca get into it. Bianca had only tussled with Amber because she was jealous. Watching Daphne passionately try to kill Amber with her bare hands was more entertaining than anything I'd seen. There was a lot of screaming and slipping as they fought each other. I wished for popcorn and had a bowl appear in my lap. I hadn't even snapped for it.

It was fun to watch, although I got tired after twenty minutes. They couldn't really hurt each other with their non-real bodies inside of the game. But some shred of conscience made me break things up after about 20 minutes of mud-wrestling. I made Amber go back into the fortress.

"Daphne," I said to a panting and angry harem member, "we have to talk about your responsibilities."

"I'm not working under that bitch," Daphne replied. "You can't make me."

"I can," I told her. "And I will." I lifted my hand to snap my fingers, but she rushed forward and held my hand still.

"Please," she begged, tears in her eyes. "Please don't make me."

She'd sworn to obey me. She was part of my harem now. But looking at the tears in her eyes, I crumbled a little bit. I had a history with Amber which meant that I was immune to some of her tricks. I'd been her doormat for way too long. But I'd still made her my First Guardian because we knew each other well. Why had I put all of my harem members in the same position I'd been in? Daphne might be a horrible bitch, but it didn't mean that I had to make her experience what I had at Amber's hands.

"I brought you here as a strategist," I told her. "So let's do that first and settle the rest later."

She was instantly happy again. I was suspicious now of the tears that she'd been about to cry; I didn't want to turn out like Dan, trapped in a loveless marriage with an angry and faithless wife. She could try to manipulate me if she wanted. She'd face consequences if she did, though. I snapped my fingers and brought her to the highest point of the fortress.

"Wow!" she exclaimed. "What a view!"

We could see the domains around us from this vantage point. "I'm going to take over our neighbors," I told her.

She was quiet for a moment. "Is this like an insane neighborhood watch grab for power?" she asked me.

"No," I responded. I looked around. "I'm going to take over all of the adjacent land."

"Kind of power hungry, aren't you?" Daphne walked towards me and touched my chest. In the real world, I would've been unable to speak and frozen in place if a woman besides Amber walked up to me and touched me like Daphne was doing. But here, I just grabbed her hand and put it on my dick.

"Power isn't the only thing I'm hungry for." I'd gotten a steady diet of virtual pussy ever since I arrived. When I wasn't trying to keep Amber happy, I was a lot happier. I wondered now if the only reason I'd proposed to her was that I couldn't imagine dying alone. Amber had taken up so much of my free time and all of the money that she could get her pretty little hands on. She had talked about the big house that she wanted to live in and the cars she wanted to have, even though my middle-class income was not really keeping up with all the stuff she wanted today, let alone tomorrow.

I snapped my fingers so that Daphne and I could do a little horizontal tango. Her hands were all over me as our lips met. She thrust her tongue into my mouth and pinched my ass.

"Sir!" Faelyn squeaked, running through the doorway. "We're under attack."

FIRST ASSAULT

"*F*uck," I swore. My boner instantly went down. I'd been collecting Guardians and handing them off to Amber to put into place. If she could handle me and a high-powered sales job, she could handle my army. Right?

Daphne motioned at herself. "Can I get some real clothes?"

As much as I liked looking at her while she was dressed like a fantasy dominatrix, I had to admit that the outfit didn't do much in terms of keeping her safe. I didn't know what happened to NPCs when they died and I didn't want to learn by one of my harem members dying. I snapped my fingers so that she was dressed like a sexy secretary, which was basically her daily outfits.

"THIS SKIRT IS GORGEOUS," she said, rubbing the fabric. "What is it made of?"

"NO TIME FOR YOUR IDIOCY," Faelyn hissed at her. "Master has to go to the command room." She looked at me expectantly. I wondered why she wasn't going back through the door when I realized she wanted me to transport us into the command room. I snapped my fingers and found complete chaos.

. . .

Amber was in her element, snapping orders at everyone. People were watching every monitor and had keyboards in their hands.

"Sir," Amber said as soon as she saw me appear. The noise abruptly cut off as if someone had hit the mute button.

"Carry on," I commanded my harem. They started talking to one another again. Amber came up and started to rattle off a ton of positions. I had a hard time paying attention, though, because somehow she'd managed to change her outfit without any of my intervention. It was a sleeveless kind of Chinese-looking dress with a high collar but a keyhole right where her cleavage was. Surreptitiously, I snapped my fingers to make the cleavage hole twice the size.

"ARE YOU EVEN LISTENING TO ME?" Amber snarled at me.

GUILTILY, I jumped just as I had whenever she used that tone of voice when I was engaged to her. Then I remembered and said, "Call me Master." I didn't threaten her with whips or chains. I didn't spank the fuck out of her. I saw her remember where we were and what she was. She knelt before me. I stroked her hair for her submissive pose, her eyes on my feet. "Try again."

"MASTER, WE'RE UNDER ATTACK."

· · ·

I ALREADY KNEW THAT. "What have you done? And this time, make it interesting."

SHE TOOK a deep breath and started over again. "All of our sectors are covered. We've kept grenades and other thing stored in caches at strategic points along the walls."

"SO YOU HAVE everything well in hand?"

"WELL..." her voice trailed off.

"WHAT HAVE YOU MISSED?" I asked, pulling her hair so that she had to look up at me.

"The twins," she gasped. "I'm sorry, sir, they're outside."

I SWORE. Of course the twins were a weak point. They were supposed to distract invading armies. I'd obviously overlooked safety measures outside of the fortress. I'd have to talk about it with Amber when we weren't actively under attack. "Where's their mother?"

"IN HERE," Amber whispered.

"DIDN'T she try to save them?"

"SHE DID," Amber agreed before she pointed. I took a look and saw that they'd hogtied the MILF to stop her from putting herself in danger to save her adopted daughters.

YIKES. While hogtying her had interesting possibilities, I had to think with something other than my dick. "Keep the invading forces away. I'll see to the twins." I snapped my fingers to go to the gate.

14 Gate of Twins

"Fuck, this bitch is the best thing I've ever had," I heard someone say. They were fucking the twins, two men per chick, and there was a line of soldiers waiting for their turns.

MY BLOOD BOILED. The twins were mine. They'd agreed to be here and be a distraction. Yes, they were by the main entrance and to some extent the distraction had worked. But I'd underestimated how many people would try to fuck them.

Leaning over the wall, I tried to snap my fingers and put them back inside where they'd be safe and the only cock they'd take would be mine, but my snapping did nothing. To my horror, my powers weren't working outside of my fortress. I remembered now that I'd had to actually walk through the forest to find my domain. I had powers inside of my caput but not outside.

"Where's your pussy master?" I heard one of them ask the twins.

. . .

"They can't answer us. Their mouths are too full." They were laughing while they rammed themselves into the two women who'd been put at the gate. I wasn't going to let my childhood play-mates be torn up by an unending train of perverts. I only had power inside of my domain. I was going to have to create things that would fling loads of flaming whatever into the line of undressing soldiers, including self-loading trebuchets and catapults. I took great pleasure in watching them scream. Some of them weren't real people, but some of them were actual players. I knew that they'd respawn somewhere else, but at least they'd think twice before showing up on my doorstep. I snapped my fingers and told Bianca, "Go untie the twins with their mom." I sent her down with their adoptive mother to the gate. I knew that the two of them would get the twins back inside the fortress as soon as they could.

As I LOOKED at them with a grin on my face, someone who was near the front of the line to fuck the twins raised his hands and chanted. My heart sank as rain started to pour. He'd put out my fucking fire. I snarled and imagined that my balls of fire were coated in gasoline. I aimed straight for him with one of my catapults, but he summoned wind to take away the flaming ball from him.

"Is THAT ALL YOU GOT?" he shouted up at me. I was handicapped by only having powers inside of my fortress. While it made sense that I couldn't use my powers elsewhere, why was he able to summon rain and wind? I needed a lot more help than I'd gotten. He was obviously on a higher level than I was.

I SET up an uninterrupted waterfall that poured off the edge of the walls. Now he looked like a drowned rat, which made me feel better. But then he called up a shitload of wind and turned my water into a tornado, which broke the wall of my fortress. Shit! I immediately fixed the wall and dismantled the tornado, but he had me shaken up.

"You SHOULD JUST SURRENDER your caput now," he sneered at me from below. "Give me your money and your women."

. . .

"YOU'RE NOT A FUCKING PIRATE, IDIOT."

"SHUT UP!" he screamed, turning red.

"WHERE'S YOUR HAREM?"

"SAFE," he grunted.

"YOU DON'T HAVE ONE, do you?" I asked. "You don't have an army."

"I DON'T NEED AN ARMY," he retorted, but I could hear the desperation in his voice.

· · ·

"You don't have your own caput, do you? You left it behind rather than be someone else's vassal."

"Shut up!" he shouted again.

"You traded for your powers, even knowing that you'd lose everything."

"I said shut up." He raised his arms and blew a bunch of fire at me. I only barely conjured water in time to counter his attack. I was able to work within my fortress but not outside of it. It was like a medieval siege and a stalemate. Any attack he focused on me would be repelled, but I was going to have to stand on the wall for a while.

. . .

It was a good thing that I didn't have to sleep, eat, drink, or anything else that I would've in the real world. He was a human being, too. It could easily get boring.

"Air, water, and fire," he shouted up at me. "Let's see if you have what it takes to counter earth."

He spread his arms. I suddenly felt like I was riding a bucking bronco in a rodeo. I nearly flew over the wall and only the presence of mind to sit down while the ground shook kept me safe. Out there, I'd be dead meat.

The earthquake went on for what seemed like forever. If he'd an army, I would've been unable to keep them from the multiple cracks in the wall that he created. But it was just him. The soldiers from the other armies had been sufficiently alarmed by the other stuff to clear out. There was no point in attacking a castle if you were going to have fire raining down on you while you tried. I didn't understand what he had done to make him so powerful, but he was still an individual. I had a team of people ready to throw grenades and shit out at attackers. I couldn't leave the wall, so I snapped Amber to me.

"DON'T FORGET TO..." she stopped. "Sir," she said when she realized I'd pulled her to the wall.

. . .

"WHAT'S THE PLAN, GORGEOUS?" She looked healthier and happier than I had ever seen her. Her cheeks were flushed and there was a glow in her eyes that I hadn't seen there in a while. Being the general to my troops, small though they were, was really good for her.

"WE STILL HAVE GRENADES EVERYWHERE. Whatever we set up is still in place, despite the earthquake. Some of our underground stores are going to have to be fixed once the fighting is over."

"WHEN DO we expect that to be? I can barely beat him off as it is."

. . .

She twisted her hands. "We have a plan."

"What is it? Why are you so nervous?"

"Sometimes, someone has to be sacrificed for the greater good."

"What do you mean?"

"We drew straws and someone got the short straw."

"Who do you plan on sacrificing?"

. . .

"FAELYN," she said. I snapped my fingers to bring Faelyn to the wall and almost absentmindedly bolstered the wall so that the tornado wouldn't rip it to shreds no matter how strong the wind got.

"MASTER, don't let them do it!" she screamed, falling at my feet. I winced at the sound her knees made when they hit the top of my stone wall. "Master, no."

"IT'S FOR THE GREATER GOOD," Amber said. "Stop sniveling."

"SHE'S UPSET. What are you talking about?"

· · ·

"WE'RE GOING to distract him by throwing a naked woman at him."

I TOOK a good look at Faelyn. She didn't have big tits, but she had cartoonishly large eyes and a very short skirt. The inch of bare skin between her skirt and socks would be very distracting.

"SOUNDS GOOD TO ME." I threw her over the wall so that she'd directly land on the asshole. I wasn't that happy about giving up one of my harem members, but if this guy was successful, he'd take them all. I would never have given up Amber or Bianca, but Faelyn was someone who basically appeared one day at the edge of my domain and was expendable. I watched as he gawked at her skirt flying up like Marilyn Monroe's had before he called a wind to lower her gently in front of him. I could see him talking to her.

"Aᴄᴛ ɴᴏᴡ," Amber said. "Send a fireball."

I ꜰᴇʟᴛ a little bad about Faelyn being in the blast zone. "I'll remember you," I called softly before I sent a giant fucking fireball over the wall to land on both of them. It was bigger than anything I'd ever seen. It was basically a miniature dwarf star.

"Nᴏᴛʜɪɴɢ ᴄᴀɴ ᴡɪᴛʜsᴛᴀɴᴅ ᴛʜᴀᴛ," Amber said, her tone approving.

· · ·

"Go back to the command room. Check that there are no other visitors." I snapped my fingers and made her go. I hoped that the twins were away from all the hubbub. A quick glance at the gate said that they'd made it out. The rain of fire had helped them at the very least.

Who knew that other players could cause earthquakes in the game? I made a mental note about getting some kind of manual. I moaned when I thought about repairing my caput. I needed to reset the walls to withstand elemental attacks like the ones that douchebag had done. I had to go out and sweep up his remains. Who knew where he'd re-spawn? I didn't want it to be on my front door. One round with him was enough. If I hadn't thrown Faelyn at him, he would've won when I got tired out. It was only luck that had helped me get through it.

My plan of attacking my neighbors seemed hopelessly stupid right now. I only had powers inside my caput. I didn't understand why my questbook had so few quests in it. Whatever that douchebag who was now a pile of ash had done, he'd had better access to his powers even when he was away from home. I needed to get rid of the ashes. I felt the temptation to call one of my harem members to deal with it, but I needed to get it far away from my domain, just in case he did respawn. From the fight that we'd had, I didn't that he could teleport. I snapped myself down to the gate with a broom and dustpan, went out the front, looked at the contraptions I'd had the twins strapped to, and walked to the giant pile of ashes that the two of them had made. I walked back into my caput and snapped myself back to Earth. I didn't want bad vibes in my own apartment, so I put them in the twins' house. That would be close enough to keep an eye on. I thought hard about whether they'd be able to respawn in the real world. Just to be sure, I put them in a small safe. They'd suffocate to death and be crushed if they respawned in there. I was more ruthless than I would be in real life, but I'd had a narrow escape. I wasn't about to tempt fate.

I SNAPPED myself back to my domain. Amber already had a list of tasks for me to do, which was something I was used to. It was a lot easier now that I could just snap my fingers and take care of things, though. They only required intention before all of the things that she wanted existed.

She finished her litany of repairs that had to be made before things were usable. Even when all it took was snapping my fingers, or especially because all it took was snapping my fingers, she had a list a mile long. I wondered if it would ever be possible for Amber to be satisfied. We were in Hell, yes, but in some ways it was Amber's Heaven. She was in charge of everybody and got to boss all of the harem members around. Frankly I was glad that she got to be the bad guy. I was fucking all of them or had plans to, anyway, and it would be awkward if I had to beat them with sticks to get them to toe the line. The idea of some BDSM made me wonder if I should take someone into a bedroom. But no. Even with all I could reconstruct with a snap of my fingers, there were other things to do. We had gotten lucky with our first attack, and now Amber was forcing everyone to listen to her in a conference room inside of the fortress. She was pointing to something on the screens which showed how we'd been breached. She seemed to have devised a multi-layer dome that would prevent intruders from dropping in on us. At the gate, there was something that looked like an airlock, the kind they used on space-ships with astronauts. I snapped my fingers and made it happen. Amber didn't even notice, high on our victory, not actually deserved and gained through luck, and her part in it. Why had I let her run my life on Earth, and why was I letting her do it again? Was it just inertia, falling back into the same old pattern over and over? Was it more comfortable to have Amber take charge than doing it myself?

I WISHED that there were actual instructions that came with this game. I felt like shit that I was one harem member down, but it couldn't be helped. If we hadn't done it, we'd have been fucked. My best plan was to move forward with fortifying the defenses in the area that I had under my control.

THEN I WONDERED why I'd made a hemisphere. Just because Amber decided something didn't mean that I had to follow her commands. I snickered to myself. I knew the perfect shape. I snapped my fingers.

· · ·

"WHAT THE FUCK!" I heard someone yelp. I grinned to myself.

"WHAT DID YOU JUST DO?" Amber asked, stomping in my direction in a way that made a ball of dread grow in my stomach. I banished it and stared her down.

"FIXED OUR DEFENSES," I replied.

"I ALREADY DESIGNED A PERFECT DESIGN."

"I'M NOT INTO IGLOOS."

. . .

SHE LOOKED AROUND. "What shape is it now?"

"GO OUTSIDE AND SEE."

SHE LOOKED at me as if she suspected a trap. But she walked outside, motioning for Bianca to come with her. Apparently Bianca was her second-in-command now. I didn't have time to look at the interpersonal dynamics in my harem, but maybe Bianca had a leg up because she had the longest relationship with Amber besides me. It didn't hurt to think about Amber cheating on me anymore. Maybe because I'd gotten the best sex of my life in Hell and was in charge now, with a whole harem of women who were willing to please me.

. . .

THERE WAS a scream of rage as soon as Amber got outside of the domain and saw what I'd done. She came in with her face redder than a tomato. "You can't do this!"

I SMIRKED AT HER. "I already did."

"THIS IS a dumb dick joke and you need to fix it. You're not an idiot scratching a dick into a bathroom door."

"OH REALLY?" I asked her, one eyebrow cocked. "I beg to differ."

. . .

"THERE ARE WOMEN HERE," she hissed at me. "What does it say if you make your harem live inside of a giant dick?"

IT WAS A MASTERSTROKE, really. So many buildings were phallic in nature, like the Eiffel Tower in the real world. Why not my fortress? "Did you notice that I put in the airlock that you thought of?" It wasn't a bad idea. It might help us stop future incursions.

"I DID NOT DESIGN A GIANT DICK," Amber screamed at me. "Fix it!"

"WATCH YOUR TONE," I told her, my voice cold as ice. "Or I can put you in a cage like Evelynn and make someone else the First Guardian."

. . .

"You can't do that," Amber sputtered. "I'm your First Guardian."

"I made you the First Guardian and I can undo it."

"By reaching back in time and acquiring someone before me?" She crossed her arms under her perfect tits.

After I tore my eyes away from her tits, I snorted. "Don't be stupid," I responded. "I don't need to travel through time." I actually thought that I might be able to. Hell and the virtual version of my memories of the real world were tenuously linked. I'd been able to travel back and forth by imagining myself to be physically located where I wanted to be.

Hadn't the experiment with Daphne and Dan taught me that I did experience time? On one hand, it'd be awesome to time travel. On the other hand, I didn't know what I could fuck up if I could go back.

I DECIDED TO TRY IT. "Gotta go. Take care of the people here."

"WAIT!" Amber screamed, but I was already gone.

SWIMMING POOL

I thought about some of the happiest memories I had as a little kid. I remembered how much fun I used to have playing with the twins next door, before everything went to shit. If I could go back in time and access my memories again, it'd be awesome. And when I'd acquired Hailey, hadn't I shown up in the Taurus I had in high school?

When I got there, I was at the pool. The twins were nowhere to be seen. I looked at my hands, which were adult sized. It was stupid to think that I could travel back in time. I turned to go and visit the MILF and twins in my domain when I heard a noise. I looked in the kitchen and saw one of their boyfriends making himself comfortable with a cold beer on the couch. I gritted my teeth. He was completely at ease, an alpha lion in his den. He had no right to be there, especially when I was the one who had all the women in this house.

I didn't have the same powers up top that I did in Hell. But that didn't mean I couldn't fuck with him. I went to the little Japanese rock garden and filled a pocket with rocks. I threw rocks at one of the windows and then snapped myself back to Hell. Then I arrived at another window and did the same thing. My long familiarity with the twins' house meant that I understood where the blind spots were. I waited for about ten minutes between each throw. By the time I hit the window with the fifth rock, I could see him on the phone. He was probably calling the police. My work was done.

I had a shred of conscience telling me that I shouldn't have freaked out the boyfriend in the house. But another part of me was smug and happy that I had the twins and their gorgeous mother to myself.

As I went back to hell, I could see Amber talking to my entire harem. Some of them were nodding. Most of them looked bored.

"Hello," I said, cutting her off. Her face was the color of a fire truck.

"Have you thought better of your rash decision, Master?" Amber snarled at me.

"No." I immediately snapped my fingers and made her disappear in a cloud of red smoke.

"Let me be clear about something," I sniffed, turning to my harem. "Amber is the First Guardian and deserves your respect and obedience. But my orders are higher than hers, and I can cancel what she says. She might be upset about the structure, but it's up to me. Is it clear?"

I heard a soft chorus of people saying yes.

"I need Daphne," I told them. "Go and do some work."

Daphne walked up to me, uncertainty on her lovely face. "You called, Master?"

"Daphne, I think Amber has gotten too big for her boots." I was going to keep Amber tied up for sensual punishment for a while. "And I think it's time that you stepped in the role I took you here for."

"Master, I don't understand." She was still dressed like a walking wet dream. I gave into my impulse to bury my face between her generous tits, the ones that had gotten her over a million dollars in the real world when she'd used them to seduce my boss. She gasped as I bit into her perfect right breast. She moaned softly while she arched her back.

"I got you here because you understand strategy. You understand the long game.

Amber is a petty tyrant, and I've made her one."

"So you're removing her as First Guardian?"

"No," I replied, toying with Daphne's buttons but actually caressing the curves of her breasts. "But I'm creating a position that is on the same level." I yanked on Daphne's hair so that her throat was exposed and started biting a trail between her ear and the center of her throat. She was breathing really hard. I wished we had the time to fuck.

"I need you to set up a strategy to invade the neighboring domains," I explained to her, whispering in her ear as she trembled in my arms. "You and I are going to conquer Hell."

Then I stood back from her, looking at the dazed expression on her face and the bite marks I'd left. They were like a work of art. They showed that I had the right to bring her to my bed and make her moan. Just looking at the bite marks was making me hard again.

"Gather information about the surrounding land and come back to me when you have a plan of attack," I ordered her. "And if you're very good, we'll see about a reward."

I was hard enough that it was uncomfortable. She looked at my erection, gave me a half grin, and walked off. I was looking forward to the next time that we had a chance to fuck. Right now, I had other fish to fry, though. I felt like I had actual responsibilities in this game now. How did that happen? Were games built to amuse people or to entangle them in a cobweb of virtual responsibilities?

I shook my head and went hunting for the place I'd taken Amber to. The second that I stepped into the room, she gave me a glare that could melt steel. "Enjoying some bondage, babe?"

I had her hands tied together with rope on a hook that was hanging from the ceiling. Her feet were barely touching the ground.

"Let me go!" she yelped.

"Naughty," I scolded. "I like you like this." I snapped my fingers and put a big ribbon bow around her throat. I put cat ears on her head.

"Let me down right the fuck now. You're going to pay for this."

"Do you think so?" I asked, snapping my fingers and making an anal plug with a cat tail appear.

"What are you doing?" Amber asked, her voice quivering a little bit. I could see that her nipples were tight points. I could see her breath coming in quick little gasps.

"Are you afraid or aroused?" I asked, even though I already knew the answer. Amber didn't answer me. I knew she was both. "If I put my fingers in your cunt right now, would you be dripping?"

"Fuck off," she snarled at me, pulling on the hook.

"You consented to become mine," I reminded her. "So when I put my fingers in your pussy and get them wet, it's with your consent."

She was glaring at me as I sank two fingers into her. As I guessed, she was dripping all over my hand. "You fucking love this." I chuckled to myself. Amber was way more kinky than I thought she was. Without giving her any warning, I spun her body around so that I could get a view of her ass.

Amber went for a run every morning, rain or shine. Seeing her get back into my apartment dripping wet had led to shower sex more than once, on the rare occasions where she let me fuck her in the morning before we worked. Her toned ass was just round enough to fill my hands.

"Do you remember the time that we shattered the shower door?"

The way that she trembled at the memory told me everything I needed to know.

"I took you from behind," I whispered. "I had my finger in your ass. Remember how full you said you felt?"

I snapped my fingers to get a bottle of lube, making sure that the anal plug was well-lubricated. "Relax," I commanded her. "Loosen up for me, or it'll hurt." She took a deep breath before I pushed it into her ass. She was as relaxed as she could get, which helped me get past her sphincter. She was breathing hard now. I didn't know if she was sobbing or not, but she was gulping for air. She wasn't even barely standing anymore. Her feet were completely off the floor while she dangled from the hook above.

I squeezed one of her beautiful tits. "Good job." I bit her ear and heard her gasp a little.

I could feel her hating me and loving this scene at the same time. I kissed the side of her unblemished neck. "You've never been more beautiful." I snapped my fingers so that she wasn't wearing anything but the anal plug, cat ears, and rope tying her wrists. I spun her on the hook again and parted her thighs. I loved the way her muscles shifted as she jumped on me, knowing that I'd catch her. The feeling of her heat pressed against me made me start to sweat a little more. When I guided myself inside of her, her breath caught. She maintained eye contact with me as I thrust inside of her, my hands on her ass, her long legs wrapped around my body. We had better sex in Hell than we'd ever had when we were above.

But why wouldn't we? We were in a virtual reality built on my memories and my own desires. I wondered how much the company would charge for a video game where every single one of your wishes came true. I guessed they'd charge out the ass. And they'd make a lot of money off of men like me, who quietly stifled in gray cubicles under fluorescent lighting.

We'd been promised things that we'd never get. Was it my dad who'd promised me that if I worked hard enough, my dreams would come true? It wasn't real. It never had been.

I was savagely fucking Amber now. I could see a hint of pain on her face mixed with the intense pleasure of having me hammer myself inside of her soft, warm cunt. She was two seconds away from orgasming. That's the second that I pulled out.

"Come back!" she screamed, panting hard, her back arched as she twisted helplessly on the hook. "I'm so close."

"It's punishment, not reward," I reminded her. I snapped my fingers and dressed in a three-piece suit. "Bye."

I vanished as she began to scream in earnest.

DAPHNE'S PLANS

I arrived just in time to see Daphne's lovely ass in the air as she leaned over a giant touchscreen. Her skirt was stretched out.

"Hi."

At the sound of my voice, she jumped a mile. She spun, her hand over her heart. "Oh my god, you scared the shit out of me."

"What are you doing there?"

"Getting everything into order." She was still talking, but I was distracted by the shoes she was wearing. I'd put them on her myself, but I hadn't looked at them when I was looking at the rest of the package. They were sky-high heels that could probably kill somebody. I could see her red-painted toenails, which must've been real because I sure as hell hadn't sent her to get a pedicure.

"Why don't you explain it to me when we're a little closer?" I sat down in a chair next to the touchscreen and patted my lap.

I could see indecision in her eyes. Even though she'd agreed to come to Hell, she didn't understand what was happening. But she sat in my lap gingerly, as if she could break something. I pulled her from the edge of my knee so that her ass was touching my erection. Daphne kept talking, but it was hard to focus when my dick was getting harder every second. I touched her clit through her tight pencil skirt, which made her buck her hips.

"Continue," I told her when she tried to turn. Her voice was no longer as confident as she described all the plans that she'd made for the invasion of our neighbors. My mind was filled with a lust-filled haze, but I still understood that she'd put together a robust plan for invading our neighbors. She'd ranked their weaknesses and strengths. She wrote down opportunities and threats, like a SWOT analysis in business school. It was easy to forget that Daphne was incredibly young, but she'd done an incredible job. I knew there was no chance that she'd done all of this by herself. She'd gotten help, but it was impressive. She had the skills that I'd believed she did. I could smell the sweet scent of her perfect hair and toyed with a lock of hair sitting on the top of her left breast. I could make her clothing disappear with a single snap of my fingers, but I liked the sensual torment of smelling her hair and feeling her warm body against mine while she struggled to keep her thoughts on the task at hand, especially while I was rubbing her clit. She was relaxing against me now, subtly pushing herself against my hand while she kept talking. There were little moans coming out of her throat now and she still was trying to focus.

When I couldn't take it anymore, I roughly got to my feet and pushed her stomach onto the touchscreen. I tore her skirt off of her, leaving destroyed a lace thong pushed to the side as I slammed inside of her body. She was as hot as an oven, writhing on my dick while her plans spun with every movement of our bodies. I put my hands around her throat, choking her a little bit. When she jerked and cried out, I felt my body find its own release. She was gasping for air when I let go of her throat.

"That was the most intense thing I've ever felt," she confessed, a hand on her throat. I'd restricted her air, which meant that her orgasm was stronger than usual.

"Dan never gave it to you like that."

"Never." She smiled at me while rubbing her throat. I didn't want to ruin the mood and talk about Xavier, so I didn't.

I snapped my fingers and got a box of wet wipes. We cleaned each other up, although Daphne's clothes were ruined. "What would you like to wear?"

"You're asking me?" Daphne seemed shocked, her eyes getting wider.

"You're on par with my First Guardian. It means that you have more power. I gave Amber the ability to decorate the fortress however she wanted. She's still hanging from a hook in a bedroom."

Daphne gulped hard.

"Anybody who crosses me will be dealt with," I explained. "But as long as you do your job right, nothing bad will happen. I didn't do anything that you didn't enjoy."

"True," Daphne admitted. I could still see the marks that I'd left on her throat. I needed to check on Evelynn at some point. I may have driven her to the brink of insanity by making her orgasm this many times.

Daphne had a beautiful flush, a perfect post-coital glow. I wanted to go another round with her, but even I needed to take a breather, even though inside of the game I could go for as long as I wanted.

"Recruit however many harem members you need, as you've outlined, and I'll check back in with you tomorrow." I snapped my finger and created a black stone.

"What's that?" Daphne asked.

"It's a way for you to call me."

"Does Amber have one?"

"No," I replied.

The smile on her face could've lit up an entire city block. "I'm the only one who has one of these?"

"Yup." She bounced towards me, her tits jiggling, right before she planted an affectionate kiss on my cheek. It was the first time that Daphne had initiated things with me. I'd had my dick inside of her, but I felt like our relationship had just reached another level. There was a strange warmth inside of my chest after being kissed on the cheek by her. "Use it responsibly."

She just waved at me and vanished. Daphne might have been a bitch when she was in a position of power over me, but I thought that it was a good idea to run after her and acquire her for my harem. She was a good strategist.

I snapped my fingers to look at Amber, who was crying now as she tried to pull the hook out of the stone ceiling above her. "I hope you've learned your lesson," I told her. I could see the tracks of tears on her cheeks which meant that she'd been crying for a while. "Untie me, you dick," she growled.

"I guess you haven't." Seeing her like this reminded me of Evelynn the Ever-Orgasmic. I snapped my fingers and left Amber behind.

Evelynn was writhing. I could see her glistening thighs. She seemed to be enjoying herself. I pulled the vibrators out of her and asked, "How do you feel?"

She groaned, "Everything is raw." I looked between her thighs. She'd been overstimulated, but even so, she was ready for more. I whipped out my dick and slid inside of her.

I'd never been inside a girl this wet before. Amber made me go down on her a lot of the time before she consented to actual fucking, and even then, she didn't get this slippery. I was sliding inside of her so smoothly that there seemed to be almost no friction. Her back was arching while she panted her way through multiple releases. It was fun to watch a woman come on my cock so frequently. It almost hurt her to climax, but I could go for a while.

"Please," she begged. "Please."

I didn't know if she wanted me to push her over the edge or not, but I started ramming her harder. With a scream, she climaxed so hard that she blacked out. Pulling out, I waited there for a few seconds, touching her to bring her back to consciousness.

"What was that?" she asked.

"Le petit mort," I told her, sliding back inside of her body.

"I can't take much more," she warned me.

"You'll take as much as I want to give you. You gave me your blanket consent for 3 years, and you have a long way to go."

I could see the pleasure mixed with sadness on her face. I had promised her what she wanted, hadn't I? She didn't seem happy about upholding her side of our agreement.

I slid a finger through her wetness before I pushed it into her ass. She was extremely relaxed and it was easy to slide one finger all the way in. Her jaw dropped as she looked at me.

"Different when it's not a toy." I leaned over and bit her left breast. "Hold on." I started hammering my hips into hers, the sound of flesh slapping together surrounding us. It was not comfortable to fuck her in this position with my fingers inside of her, so I turned her over. Then I could easily fuck her and keep my finger in her ass.

I had done something to her by making her orgasm until I felt like taking the vibrators away. She could last for much longer than any of the other girls in my harem. I didn't know what else she could do now, but I wanted to find out. White-hot flames flooded my body as she took a release that lasted longer than the ones I'd had with Daphne or any of the other girls. She was covered in fluids now. I made sure she could move freely before I handed her a box of wet wipes, too. "Clean yourself up."

She gingerly touched herself between her thighs. I could see her swollen clit begging for attention even after all of that. "Do you want me to send someone in here to tend to you?"

"No," she said. "But I wouldn't mind some food."

"What do you want?" After giving me an orgasm like the one I'd just had, she could have anything.

"Maine Lobster," she said.

I snapped my fingers and got her lobster without the shell next to mustard and butter sauce. She ate like she was starving, although of course she wasn't. I stroked her head as I watched her eat. I probably should've taken away the vibrators earlier, but it was hot to watch her orgasm again and again. Maybe it would be important later on. I kissed her buttery lips once before I left her alone once more.

When I arrived in the bedroom where Amber was, her head was hanging down. She wasn't even crying anymore, defeat in every line of her body.

"How do you feel?"

"I'm sorry, Master."

I took a moment to absorb her apology. She rarely if ever apologized. I had to savor this moment.

"For what?"

"For undermining you." Misery was all over her face. "Please accept my apology."

"Apology accepted," I said. "But I'm not done with you." With a snap of my fingers, I had a bowl of ice in my hand. I unhooked her hands and put her on the bed.

"What's happening?" Amber asked while I made sure her hands were attached to the metal headboard.

"You'll see." I slid an ice cube down her body, touching her nipples until they were hard, and then licking up the water that they left behind. I eventually pushed one inside of her body with my tongue, which made her yelp beneath me. I sucked it out and kept pushing it back in.

"Your tongue feels like it's made of fire," she moaned. "I don't know if I can handle it."

"You can," I said when the ice cube was inside of her. She was beyond words when I slid my tongue into her pussy to suck the ice cube back into my mouth. I stood up and pinched her jaw open, pushing the pussy-soaked ice cube into her mouth. She moaned as the ice cube melted in her hot mouth. Then I put my hands in her hair and sealed our mouths together, playing tonsil hockey. Amber never let me kiss her like this because she said that it triggered her gag reflex, the same reason why she rarely gave me head. Now that I had her tied up, she couldn't do much. And maybe inside of the game, there were no such things as gag reflexes. Or the need to actually breathe.

When I was done, I pulled back. She looked stunned. "Fuck, why haven't we done this before?"

There were a lot of answers to that question. She'd taken control in the bedroom every time we got naked, which was hot at first but got old quickly. I didn't mind having her ride my cock like she was about to die tomorrow, but I also liked to fuck her face down, ass up, with handcuffs on and the opportunity never presented itself.

Well, until now.

I smiled as I made handcuffs appear. I made sure that she was facedown on the mattress. I snapped my fingers and got a whip in my hand. She couldn't even see me raise my hand, but she jumped as soon as the whip touched her gorgeous ass. The yelp that came out of her was the loudest sound she had probably made in her life.

Another day, I'd have the patience to turn virtual Amber's ass totally pink. Right now, though, I was going to do something that she'd never let me have. I slid two fingers inside of her cunt, testing her. She was ready to be pounded so hard we'd probably break the headboard.

The second that I slid inside of her, I could feel her trying to milk me. Her muscles were fluttering like crazy around my dick. I clenched my teeth and held myself still, but she had other plans. She was moving as much as she could, backing up so that she could take more of my cock inside of her. It turned out that she liked this position, too. I put my hands on her shoulders so that I control the speed and depth of the thrusting. Her voice was muffled but I knew she was enjoying herself from the way that her juices were starting to slide down her thighs.

My balls drew up a split second before I came inside of her. Amber didn't like it raw normally. Now I had filled her up with so much semen that it was joining her juices, leaving trails on her thighs as everything hit the sheets.

I got rid of her handcuffs and slid my hand through our combined come. "Open," I told her. I fed her my come. I fed her her own come. I fed her our come. And despite being initially reluctant to lick it up from my hand, she did it anyway. She was learning to obey me.

I snapped my fingers as took us into a shower, where I cleaned up her body before I cleaned up mine. I snapped again to make the bed so perfectly made that you could bounce a quarter off of it. Amber leaned in and rested her head on my shoulder.

"I love you."

Three words that she used to get her way in real life. She pulled it out during arguments, telling me she loved me, but she couldn't stand X behavior. I'd given up going to LAN parties on Friday nights because she didn't like being alone. I didn't play poker with the boys because she hated gambling, even harmless gambling where no real money was involved. I rarely got to go to happy hours with anybody but Xavier, and only then for a little bit.

It was different to hear them from her in Hell. She'd used her so-called love to control me and basically destroy my life. Now she was trying to manipulate me and solidify her position.

"Listen to me," I said, trying to be stern but still feeling good from fucking her and then cleaning her up. I rested my chin on the top of her head, her soft hair tickling my chin a little. "I've given you a tremendous amount of power here. I don't want you to abuse it. This place is mine."

"I know," she said, her voice muffled as she turned her head and kissed the base of my throat, which made my cock pretty happy. "I'm sorry for being upset about the building."

"It's not about the architecture," I countered, feeling the curve of her ass, the indent of her waist, and the sides of her boobs, which were slightly wider than her frame. "It's about respecting me and understanding why you're here."

"Why am I here? I don't mind the sex, but I'm rallying people for what?"

"I'm a laird out here."

"What? I didn't know that you were Scottish."

"I'm not. Well, maybe. I don't know, it's a question to ask a genealogist or some shit. I have to defend my caput, and you're vital for that."

"What's a caput?"

"My fortress." I let my hand drift to her ass and squeezed a handful before pulling her away. "You're important here. But don't let that blind you from your purpose."

"What happens if you lose the caput?"

"I'll become the vassal of the person who conquered me."

I could see a calculating gleam in her eye. "It has to be another laird. You can't just stage a coup and take over the caput as a member of my harem."

"Oh," she said, her face falling. I thought that we'd come to an accord over her part in my life. However, she seemed like she was trying to figure out a way to get out of here.

"You agreed to be here. Do you want me to release you from that vow?" I liked the rough sex we'd been having, the kind of sex that left marks on both of our bodies, but I wasn't going to keep a First Guardian who was trying to undermine me every second of the day.

"No," she said. "I want to be with you."

She was like a beautiful viper, entrancing and deadly. I was having second thoughts about having Amber in here. Daphne could serve the same function.

I'd give it a little more time, I decided. She was not ready to be completely on her own. But the girls listened to her, which counted for a lot.

"Sweetheart," I said to her. "I want you to talk to Daphne about your part in her plans for our security."

I could see a flash of anger cross her brow. "Yeah, okay." She didn't sound enthusiastic at all. She acted like a prisoner going to death row. I watched her shuffle off.

Fuck, I thought that keeping a bunch of women who were happy to slide onto my dick would be fun. It was one of my ultimate fantasies, along with a giant pool and unlimited drinks. Now I was stressed out about the relationships that the girls had with one another as they clawed their ways to the top. I understood why there were so many books about political intrigue. As soon as you put a bunch of chicks in one place, they'd jostle for position. With guys, you'd probably decide the hierarchy by having people wrestle each other into submission. I looked at my virtual body. Probably part of the draw of the game was that I had the body of a Greek god without the associated gym time or having to be obsessed with what I ate. I liked eating bread and pasta. After late nights at the office, sometimes I'd go to this famous hot dog place that was around the corner and eat one of those. Amber gave me shit about chemicals or something but I didn't come home half of the time, since she was always on the road.

Why had I accepted a half life? Was it because I'd been on a road and never questioned the path that I'd followed, the one chosen for me by parents and teachers? Why had I never reached out for the things that I wanted for myself?

This video game was making me question a lot of things that I'd chosen. When I was a little kid, I had little kid dreams. I wanted to be a race car driver. I wanted to become an astronaut. I wanted to change the world.

As an adult, I'd agreed to be so much less. Why? I swallowed hard, facing some ugly truths about how I'd conformed and lost all of my dreams. Nowadays, my wedding to Amber, who was out of my league, was the best thing. And Amber was a nightmare. In what world was that the best thing that could happen to me?

After I got out of this video game, I needed to make some major life changes. I'd broken up with Amber, but the next place that I decided to work, it was going to help my own life goals. I was done with working for other people and putting cash in their pockets. I needed to build up the skills to reach out and make my own way.

I didn't know why being placed in a position of illusory power was making me feel this way. Maybe by the time I got back to the real world and finished testing the game, I'd feel differently. But somehow, I thought that the lesson would stick with me.

I wanted to be alone. I liked having fuckable girls around all the time, but the weird harem politics were kind of a drag. I knew that I couldn't spend that much time in the virtual world above because I had responsibilities. I made a mental note to tell them that having to oversee major goals was kind of a bummer. Coordinating people was like something out of a nightmare. Xavier had once said that managing people was like herding cats.

He was right. I accidentally fell into a management position as a demonlaird and it kind of sucked.

Who knew that having a harem full of horny women would be so complicated? I was about to say "Fuck it." I was over the stressful parts of this game. But then my ear rang.

BLACK STONE

I tugged on my ear. It kind of felt like the way that your ears burned when people were talking about you, but it was a lot louder. I tugged harder on my ear.

"Master," Daphne called. "Are you there?"

Holy shit. So this was what the black stone did.

"Yup," I said to her, wondering if I needed a microphone or something.

"You need to come back to the caput right now." The tone of her voice said that it was urgent.

I snapped my fingers. There were sirens going off all over the place. "What is it?" I asked Daphne.

"I was preparing our first force to go out when all the alarms started going off." Daphne wrapped her arms around me, as if she needed comfort. I stroked her hair while she continued, "And we're being attacked."

I saw a face on the screens that I hoped to never see again.

"Fuck. He re-spawned." The douchebag who had the mix of elemental powers anywhere had shown up with a disciplined army this time. There was no ragtag band of idiots distracted by fucking the flawless adopted sisters who looked like twins. He had come for me with a vengeance.

Apparently locking him away hadn't turned out well. Then my heart stopped as I looked at the person flying next to him, her feet not touching the ground. "Is that Faelyn?"

Daphne squinted. "Maybe?"

I needed Amber right now. I snapped my fingers and made sure that she was wearing a black suit with nothing under it. Her hair was in the kind of twist that I was pretty sure required magic to keep up. She looked like a general or something, but she also wasn't wearing a bra. Not for the first time, I wondered if my fantasies somehow were changed by the people I was fantasizing about. There were details that I wouldn't have dreamt up.

"Ready to go?" I asked Amber.

"I was born ready." She licked her lips and trailed one hand down my arm, sending a death glare at Daphne, who was still clinging to me like I was the only safe harbor in a storm.

"Let's go," I told her. I'd implemented a lot of what Amber had wanted in the design of this place. Sure, it wasn't a multi-entry igloo, but it wasn't as vulnerable as the medieval fortress it used to be. I snapped my fingers to bring Evelynn to the underground levels and checked every entry point. They'd have a much harder time getting in.

"Bar the doors," Amber urged. There were only three doors and one secret underground tunnel. The tunnel could've been a point of vulnerability if more than one person knew about it. Amber didn't even know, and she'd designed the rest. I put giant blocks of steel, resistant to a lot of things including that asshole's magical powers, in front of every door. There was a false door at the tip of the dick, but it was filled with lava and an electrical fence beneath the layer of lava. They could try to climb on top of the giant dick, but they wouldn't be able to break it. I wanted to smell their bodies thoroughly cooked by lava and electricity as they tried to get inside of my fortress. Turned out that I was a lot more bloodthirsty than horny, after the initial rush of gathering my Guardians.

I made sure that there were motion detectors that would immediately throw lava at anybody trying to enter my secret tunnel or walk through it. I also sent my neighbors down there so that they could sound the alarm. They couldn't move through the tunnel; I had a surveillance room specifically for it so that they could sit there, inside of a steel case, and tell me if something was happening. Unlike Daphne, they didn't get a direct line. They would only get a telephone that'd ring in the command room.

I didn't want to put them with the others, because then the secret tunnel would no longer be a secret. Amber knew that there was something out there, but my ability to snap my three neighbors in and out of a sealed steel room meant that they couldn't direct anybody to the tunnel even if they tried. I'd been careful to check that the upgrades in cameras all over did not hit my secret escape route. I had set up the cameras with a snap of my fingers to a feed that I controlled. But I couldn't be everywhere at once during an invasion, which was why I had harem members.

I made sure that Daphne and Amber had what they needed. Both of them were dressed in what I thought of as fuck-me-black clothing. They basically looked like lunchtime nooners. They were directing my troops according to the security plans they'd already drawn up. Even though I'd just punished Amber, I knew that she would be more than capable of doing her job.

I snapped my fingers and went to the tip of the dick. I smiled to myself, even though there was nobody to see me, while I listened to my lava kill someone dumb enough to try to climb inside of the dick. When his body was thoroughly charred, the electric fence caught it. It kind of smelled like roast pig at a luau but the smell was stronger. I made a bottle of something like Febreze appear in my hand to get rid of the worst of the smell. I'd never smelled a cooked human or cooked virtual human before, but it wasn't exactly a pleasant odor.

Then I remembered that I could do anything out here. I encased myself in a full-body suit, like an astronaut or a knight. Inside of the suit, there was a controlled air system that had good air filters. They apparently hadn't gotten communications from the first guy, because I could hear a second guy going into the lava. Then a third.

Then as I heard a thump, I realized that the third guy had used the second guy as a slowly sinking platform and was reaching for the electric layer that was below the layer. He was pulling himself onto it. He must be wearing some kind of non-conductive suit that was protecting him from being fried. They had learned about the lava, and this was their second attempt to penetrate. I casually made some knives appear out of thin air. I could hear his screams as I slashed through his suit and his bare skin was exposed to the electrified layer that he'd thought to overcome. Maybe if there hadn't been anybody up here, he would've been successful.

It was time to utilize another member of my harem. I snapped my finger and made Evelynn appear. She was no longer in her box. I snapped my fingers again to put her in a knife-proof nonconductive suit.

"Hey, babe." I looked her up and down. Most of the guys who worked on the power lines had never looked as sexy as she did. Yeah, most of her skin was covered, but of course I'd fitted the suit to her body. She kind of looked like a superhero, if female superheroes were there to murder intruders.

"What is this place?"

"Welcome to Just the Tip," I said, winking when she laughed.

"Am I the only one who gets to enjoy the Tip?" she asked coyly.

"Well, you would know all about Tips, eh?"

She only snorted and gave me the finger. "Yeah, I guess I would." She spun in a slow circle. "It's bigger than it looked from down there."

"Yeah, it's pretty far away. It's hard to see the scale."

"I knew that the base was wider, but it's still pretty big up here." We both heard the screams of someone melting inside of the lava. I wondered what happened to the bodies of the people who went in there. Obviously, they burned to death, but my lava pit might overflow. I snapped my fingers to make the sides of the lava pit even higher. I didn't want more people using rapidly sinking bodies as stepping stones as the guy I'd fried after cutting his suit did.

"What exactly do you want me to do here?" She snapped her fingers and nothing happened. "I don't have a lot of powers."

"Come here," I said. She walked in front of me and put her hands on my hips, drawing me closer to her. Another hand went to the back of my head so she could pull me down for a kiss. I knew that orgasming and being part of a public art display had changed her confidence. She knew that she was hot shit.

Back when she was a waitress dealing with average pervs, she had kind of rolled her eyes when random dudes grabbed her ass. But she wasn't some random blondie at Hooters who got paid to be ogled at a breastaurant. She didn't understand the kind of power that hot women had over men, who were visual creatures. Her mouth tasted like sugar when she kissed me.

I had to pull away. "Stop distracting me. We have to make sure nobody gets in through the roof. It's a false door, but it's still possible for people to get through."

"What do you want me to do?" Evelynn asked. "Flash my tits at them?"

My mind was temporarily distracted by the thought of a topless Evelynn stunning the incoming men before killing them. It was hot to think of her as a femme fatale, a Bond girl with a gun behind her back. I snapped a couple guns into existence.

"Those are too big. Those are the kinds of guns that guys get when they have to compensate for something." Evelynn shook her head, although there was kind of a gleam in her eye while she looked at guns that were almost as long as she was tall.

"I'm not giving you a pea shooter to defend the Tip."

"How about some shotguns?"

"Sawed-off?"

"Sure." I could tell that she didn't know much about guns, but I snapped my fingers and put two shotguns in her hands.

"You need some target practice," I said. I snapped my fingers and put military-grade sights on her shotguns. Yeah, they weren't sniper rifles, but they could do the job if I enhanced them to have extreme accuracy inside of my fortress. There were more people coming through the top of the Tip. I snapped my fingers and put us on a platform safely away from the opening but close enough that she could shoot.

"This is the best," she said, as blood flew everywhere while she shredded the invaders. Some came with suits and some didn't, meaning that they were from different armies. All of them tried to jump over the lava, and only some of them made it. I'd set up auto-stabbing knives that came out of nowhere once douchebags thought they were safe. Before they died, she used them for target practice.

It took a few minutes to figure out how to use the sights on her shotguns. It was pretty short range practice, but she was going to be in an enclosed space. I put very light-weight bulletproof armor on her. I also needed to give her a panic button. I might not always be able to come to her side if she needed help, but there were a bunch of chicks in the building.

"Do you want to be here by yourself?" I asked her. "You want a friend?"

"A girl?" she asked as she shot some poor asshole five times in the chest as he died in front of us, slowly sinking into the lava.

"Yeah."

"Sure, I guess," she said.

I knew that Bianca was a good fit for someone who already would take the lead. Bianca would do anything I asked her to do. I snapped my fingers. She was dressed in battle gear and looked like the hottest military recruit on Earth.

"Why am I here, Master?"

"What does Daphne have you doing?" I asked her.

"I'm doing perimeter patrol."

"Great, so you can do perimeter patrol here." I saw her kind of gasp. "Am I fucking up Daphne's plans?" She hesitated to tell me yes.

I should've checked out the details of Daphne's plan. I snapped my fingers and put Bianca back in place. I told Evelynn, "Stay here and kill any intruders."

She gave me a bloodthirsty grin before shooting someone right in the center of his mass a second later. I wondered if giving her a gun was the best idea before finding my way to the command center. I needed to pick up Daphne's plans and see how the rest of things were going.

When I got there, Amber was firmly in charge, her hair perfect while she kept her eyes on the cameras we had stationed everywhere. Daphne was standing beside her. I could see the tension in both of their bodies. There were harem members crawling all over strategic points inside of the balls of the building.

I felt like they didn't need me there. I also didn't see any harem members just sitting around. I realized that Evelynn wasn't part of their plans because they must not consider her an asset.

"Is there anything you need me for?" I asked Daphne and Amber.

"No," they said in unison.

"Bye," I snapped my fingers. I guessed that Evelynn wouldn't have a friend. Faelyn might've been part of it if she weren't outside. How much did she know about me anyway? She knew what I liked, but I had completely revamped the fortress since she left. I'd addressed the worst security risks. As soon as I thought that, a set of alarms started going off. I put my hands over my ears.

"Are you okay?" Evelynn asked. Then I realized that the alarms were inside of my head, just like when Daphne called for me. But she would be talking to me, not setting off alarms.

My neighbors. They were in trouble in the secret tunnel.

DEFENDING THE TUNNEL

*T*could snap my fingers and appear in the control room instantaneously. The three of them were safe, but the screens told another story.

"Oh, no," I murmured, looking at the number of soldiers who had apparently found their way into the tunnel. "This won't do at all."

"What are you talking about?" One of the twins laid her hand on my chest and leaned in. "What will you do?" It was a purr. I could see in her eyes that she was aroused by the idea of me killing everyone. I had no idea that the twins were so bloodthirsty.

"Get back here," her mother growled. She was still pissed that I'd fucked both of her adopted daughters.

I snapped my fingers and filled the tunnel with molten lava. The screaming coming from the speakers was very loud. The three women in the control room down by the secret tunnel clamped their hands over their ears and closed their eyes. I only laughed.

Who laughed when they heard the death cries of an invading force? Me, apparently. Something inside of this game had changed me in a fundamental way. I was already sad, thinking about when this was all over and I went back to my real life, where I had no power, tons of responsibilities, and extra shit from the women in my life.

But right now, I could see that the tunnel had not turned everyone back. I sealed it with tons of granite, letting it fall and crush anybody stupid enough to be in the tunnel. It was shame that I couldn't save any to question.

"Come here," I told the twin who'd put her hand on my chest. I pulled her mouth to mine, stroking her silky hair while I pushed my tongue in her mouth.

"Gross," her mom said, turning away. I wondered if she'd understood how stifled her daughters had felt as professional cheerleaders. They were hot, yeah, but they were overworked and underpaid. I vaguely remembered some lawsuit about cheerleaders being paid less than minimum wage for the time that they put in. I was able to give them anything topside in this game. I could make them billionaires with a twitch of my fingers. Because it amused me, I put a billion dollars into three accounts for all of them. When they returned and left my domain in Hell, they'd be well provided for.

I flicked my wrist and sent a camera zooming through the tunnel on the other side. I could hear the quiet whimpers as people died. What was this game? It gave me the power of a dark god and a macabre delight in death. I wasn't this person. I'd cried when my dog died when I was 8. He was my best friend. But I was more than willing to stomp all these NPCs into oblivion. Hell, I even was happy to stomp real players in PvP mode.

I went to look at the three of them, who were whispering. Their mom basically looked like a tomato. I sauntered up and asked, "Trouble, ladies?"

"I want you to take us home," their mother blurted out. "I want to get out of here. I know what you've been promised. My daughters will serve you... but above-ground. Not in this weird hellhole in a building shaped like a giant dick."

I didn't take orders from any woman. "I'm afraid I can't let you do that. You all promised me to obey my orders."

She glared at me. I was surprised I didn't spontaneously combust. It was super hot to get yelled at by the MILF next door about staying away from her beautiful daughters. I was getting hard with every moment. Angry sex with her would be really fun.

With a snap of my fingers, I changed her outfit so that she was wearing a see-through push-up bra that made her breasts spill over the cups. She was wearing a tiny thong. And her wrists were handcuffed together.

"What the fuck?" she exclaimed.

"I think you've forgotten who is in charge. I own you," I responded. I could see her two adopted daughters watching us with interest. With another snap of my fingers, I had placed something metal inside of her mouth that forced it open. With another snap of my fingers, my cock was in her mouth. I couldn't fundamentally alter people without using points, but I could change their outfits with a thought. I could see the twins staring at their mom's ass. I knew that they'd never viewed their mother as a sexual object, but I certainly had. I put a proprietary hand around her neck. I'd wanted to do this for decades. She definitely knew how to blow like a professional. I was about to shoot just a minute after she began. I forced my cock down her throat as I came and made her swallow. She looked a little dazed as I pulled my dick out of her mouth.

Then the training module showed up. Luci looked as fine as ever, clad in a red suit that showed tons of cleavage. She wasn't wearing anything under the suit jacket, not even a bra. I was distracted by the movement of her perfect breasts.

"Well, as entertaining as this has been, I'll probably stop you now. You've won your first victory, which means that you've completed your first round."

"What happens next?" I asked.

"Good question. You wanna see your contract?"

Was this part a standard piece of the training module?

"Read here."

I, the undersigned, sign my soul to the care of Lucifer.

"I mean, it's just a game. Nobody ever expects for any EULA to be enforced."

"Don't you know what they say about deals with the devil?" Luci purred. She walked up to me and put her hand on my chest. I was starting to get scared but incredibly horny at the same time. My brain was sending me conflicting signals.

"I want to get out of this game. I want to go home."

"Oh sweetie," Luci replied, shaking her head. "I own your soul now. You're going to be one of my faithful hellhounds, just like Rufus."

I started to sweat. Rufus was a guy who'd been transformed into a hellhound?

"Do I have any other options?"

"Well, just one. You can keep your caput and your harem if you do one little thing for me. And I'll set up a laser perimeter to stop anybody from getting into your little barony. You'll never be able to grow it, but if you're happy with the space you have for your women, that's all that matters."

"My fortress is fine."

"Then you have one out: you get 24 hours to have one of your friends sign over his soul to me."

I had to doom someone else eternally in order to get out of being a hellhound? "What kind of option is that? I'm not that much of a dick, not now that I know what's going on and who you really are."

She smiled like a cat who got the cream. "I think you are that much of a dick." She caressed my penis. "And don't worry, sometimes I transform my hell-hounds back into men so I can have fun."

It sounded like the difference between getting someone else to take my place was being enslaved as a hellhound or getting autonomy and living as a baron. It was a no-brainer, in the end. There were two bad options.

"Take me to the surface."

"I thought you'd say that." She flicked a finger, and the world around me dis-solved into red smoke.

MALL

I was back in the mall where Gareth had found me. I was, unbelievably, wearing the same clothes that I'd been wearing when I'd gone into the video game test room and accidentally signed away my soul to Lucifer. I saw one of my high school friends passing by.

"Hudson!" I yelled out. He turned to look at me. "Hey man, haven't seen you in a while. What've you been up to?"

He looked like he'd been crying or had severe allergies. "Not much."

"There's this new video game that I want you to play. I know how much fun we had in high school playing in Gareth's basement."

"I don't know... I don't really feel like doing much."

"Just try out this new video game. It won't take that long."

"Sure. Fine." Hudson walked slowly behind me. I breathed a sigh of relief. If I could get his name on the dotted line, I wouldn't have to spend eternity as a hellhound.

When we walked into the office, Luci literally was glowing. I didn't know if I would notice if I didn't know who she was, but now that I did, the satanic grin gave everything away.

"Hi! I'm Luci."

I watched Hudson fumble over his words as he was confronted by the ultimate male fantasy.

"Before we get started, we just have a few pieces of paperwork..."

I could tell that Hudson couldn't even really hear her talking. He was mesmerized by her low-cut top, the same way that I had been. It was almost too easy to convince him to stick around. I watched him take the pen and sign away his soul, just as quickly and easily as I had. The moment that he finished signing the contract, Luci made me transport straight back to my caput. I was looking forward to some hot tub time with as many gorgeous women who could fit into the hot tub of my dreams.

THE END

www.ingramcontent.com/pod-product-compliance
Lightning Source LLC
Chambersburg PA
CBHW020251030726
47499CB00001B/150